The Case of the General's Thumb

Andrey Kurkov was born in St Petersburg and now lives in Kiev. He studied at the Foreign Language Institute in Kiev and worked for some time as a journalist. He spent his military service as a warder in Odessa prison. Later he became a film cameraman and now writes screenplays, including of his own work. He has published ten novels, including *Death and the Penguin*, and four books for children.

George Bird has translated extensively from Russian and German. In 1986 he won the Pluto Crime Prize for his novel *Death in Leningrad*.

ALSO BY ANDREY KURKOV

Death and the Penguin
Penguin Lost

Andrey Kurkov

THE CASE OF THE
GENERAL'S THUMB

TRANSLATED FROM THE RUSSIAN BY
George Bird

VINTAGE

Published by Vintage 2004

2 4 6 8 10 9 7 5 3 1

Copyright © 1999 by Andrey Kurkov and
Diogenes Verlag AG Zurich
English translation copyright © George Bird 2003

Andrey Kurkov has asserted his right under the Copyright,
Designs and Patents Act, 1988 to be identified as the author
of this work

First published in 2000 with the title
Igra v otrezanny palets by
FOLIO, Kharkov and Moscow

First published in Great Britain in 2003 by
The Harvill Press

Vintage
Random House, 20 Vauxhall Bridge Road,
London SW1V 2SA

Random House Australia (Pty) Limited
20 Alfred Street, Milsons Point, Sydney
New South Wales 2061, Australia

Random House New Zealand Limited
18 Poland Road, Glenfield,
Auckland 10, New Zealand

Random House (Pty) Limited
Endulini, 5A Jubilee Road, Parktown 2193,
South Africa

The Random House Group Limited Reg. No. 954009
www.randomhouse.co.uk

A CIP catalogue record for this book
is available from the British Library

ISBN 0 09 945525 0

Papers used by Random House are natural, recyclable
products made from wood grown in sustainable forests.
The manufacturing processes conform to the environ-
mental regulations of the country of origin

Printed and bound in Denmark by
Nørhaven Paperback, Viborg

THE CASE OF THE
GENERAL'S THUMB

1

Kiev, night of 20th–21st May, 1997

Sergeant Voronko of the State Vehicle Inspectorate loved his snug little glass booth on Independence Square in the heart of Kiev, and never more than in the small hours, when Khreshchatik Street was free of traffic, and nipping out for a smoke was to experience a vibrant, blanketing silence very different from the fragile night stillness of his home village. Kiev lay open before him, not frightening as to most at that hour, but stirring feelings of affection and pride. He was its protector, security officer, bodyguard; solicitous proprietor of a vast and varied domain embracing the Central Post Office, the fountains, even the red Coca-Cola balloon tethered near where the Lenin monument once stood.

At 1.30 a.m. he got out his laptop, a token of gratitude from a Tax Police friend for supplying documentation for a top-range Opel Kadett illegally imported from Germany. A small favour between friends, which is, after all, what friends are for.

So, to the nocturnal enjoyment of Khreshchatik Street *deserta*, he now added that of playing cards with the computer, and since it was just a computer, no shame attached to losing. The hand it dealt him tonight was a peach, but no sooner had he played his first card than a bulb on the panel in front of him flashed and a tinny *Seven! Proceed at once to Eleven!* intruded on the peace and quiet of the booth.

Voronko acknowledged the message, slipped the laptop into his briefcase, and set off in his SVI Zhiguli.

Post 11 was Pechersk, reasonably close. He could be there and back, and still get a few hands of cards in before his relief arrived.

1

He had not been gone five minutes when the Coca-Cola balloon heaved itself slowly up into the Khreshchatik Street sky, and dangling from it was a body.

Seven! Attendance no longer required. Return to post, Tinny Voice instructed over the car radio as Pechersk Bridge came in sight.

Shaking his head in disbelief, Voronko performed a u-turn and made his way back to Khreshchatik Street and the prospect of three hours' cards.

2

Kiev, 23rd May, 1997

"A rest's what you need, Nik," Ivan Lvovich observed as they drew away from the station in a dark blue BMW.

It was true, after seven days' travel on top of a hectic month selling a flat, packing and seeing off a container of family effects.

Tadzhikistan now seemed remote, alien. Tanya and Volodya were safe with relatives in Saratov, where it would be pleasant enough now, in summer, with the Volga to swim in or fish, and good Slav faces around instead of the furtive, unsmiling Tadzhik variety.

"Kiev can wait," said Ivan Lvovich. "First, a spell of recuperation at a nice little place with all mod cons. And while you're there I can brief you."

The "nice little place" recalled Granny's chalet with garden near Zhitomir, where Nik had spent whole summers with his mother until his parents' deaths in '65. From then on home was with his father's people in distant Dushanbe. There he finished his schooling, and graduated from the Institute of Military Interpreters. After a spell at HQ Military District, two postings to Africa. On his return, marriage to Tanya. They had a son, Volodya, and all had gone well until Tanya's sacking by a boss who took

Independence to mean a Geological Scientific Research Institute cleansed of non-Tadzhiks. Later, he rang and apologised. Anyway, they'd be better off in Russia, he said. But would they? Dumped in Saratov, like Tanya and Volodya, on folk with scarcely a kopek to their name?

His chancing to meet Ivan Lvovich had been most fortunate. He'd been coming from Border Guards Admin., seething at having his transfer to Russia refused, when a middle-aged colonel asked the way to the Hotel for Officers, and he'd offered to show him. As they walked, they talked.

That evening, over a meal in a Turkish restaurant, Ivan Lvovich mentioned a new Service being created in Ukraine, and the possibility of getting in at an early stage, especially given the plus of a Zhitomir granny. There would, of course, be help with move and accommodation, though it would take time to organize.

"Beer drinker?" Ivan Lvovich asked, as they shot out into a blaze of sunlight on the river embankment.

"Yes."

"Stop at the crayfish," Ivan Lvovich ordered the driver, spotting a cardboard notice, two buckets, and a young man on a collapsible stool in swimming trunks and sun glasses.

"How much?"

"Fifty kopeks each."

"I'll have twenty."

Ten minutes later they were clear of the city, in a lofty pine forest.

Nik thought suddenly of his friend Lyoshka's "Life is Chance", a dictum never far from his lips, until Zaire, where his, not Nik's, was the vehicle that went over the land mine.

"That's it," said Ivan Lvovich indicating a Finnish chalet approached by a gravel path. "Old Party-high-up retreat."

It had three rooms, a kitchen and a veranda.

"Saucepan for the crayfish, beer from the fridge, and we're in business," said Ivan Lvovich.

Going through to the bedroom, Nik rummaged through his

cases for the leather-wrapped antique Turkish *yataghan* bought in a Samarkand market.

"A small gift for getting us here," he said, presenting it to Ivan Lvovich.

"Bloody hell!" he exploded, brandishing the elegantly curved blade. "This in your kit all the way from Dushanbe! They only had to find that at any one of the frontiers and your feet wouldn't have touched!"

"Sorry," Nik said wearily. "It couldn't go in the container – containers get the full treatment – and I didn't want to ditch it."

"Anyway, thank you, Nik. We've been lucky."

He poured beer.

"Lovely thing. It'll go well with my wall carpet. I'm sorry, too. Still a bit on edge. Worried we might be under observation. But happily, Security's up to its eyes. Some clever sod's used an advertising balloon to dump a corpse on their roof. Twenty surveillance cameras and not one looking skywards! Balloon hanging. Something of a novelty. And some corpse! Retired general, Presidential Defence Adviser."

"Why knock off an old chap like him?"

"Old chap be damned! Forty-seven. Early retirement. State Security, then Min. of Def. – where one year's desk counts as three of actual service. So it's him we have to thank for smoothing our arrival!"

They clinked glasses.

"Now for the crayfish."

Half an hour later Ivan Lvovich left, saying Nik should have a good rest, and he'd be back in a day or two.

Nik drank another beer, took a shower, and drawing the curtain of the tiny window, lay on the wide bed, and to the rhythmical swaying of a train, fell asleep.

3

It was a fine, starry night, and Viktor Slutsky made short work of the long, lonely walk from the metro station to his high-rise block of flats. In contrast to most tenants of the month-old block, he walked without fear, brand-new warrant card in his pocket, Tula Tokarev automatic holstered under his arm. He'd had, to date, no occasion to produce either, on duty, or walking this tortuous kilometre of building sites. The curious logic of starting to build at a point furthest from the metro eluded him. But at least he, Ira and their three-month-old daughter were no longer cooped up in a hostel.

Now, up to the eighth floor, and supper. The lift had yet to be installed, a fact for which tenants, except perhaps the elderly couple on the twelfth floor, were physically the fitter. Pause to accustom his eyes to the dark.

Hearing his key in the lock, petite, peroxided, teenager-like Ira looked out into the corridor, carrying their daughter.

"Remembered the butter?"

His cheerful smile vanished.

"Plain potatoes for you then," she said calmly. "And when fat's what you need, being so thin."

"Is there any?"

"There's lard, in the freezer."

"Let's have that."

Ira returned Yana to her pram, and they sat down at the kitchen table.

Viktor ate in silence. Lard and potatoes, he reflected, might be the more palatable for frying, though this was not the right moment to say so.

"Come on, out with it," Ira prompted, seeing Viktor still wearing the ghost of a smile.

"I've been given a case."

"When's the ration hand-out?"

"That's all you care about," sighed Viktor. "Actually, there's butter tomorrow, a whole kilo."

"What else?"

"The usual: buckwheat, condensed milk, tinned herring . . ."

For a while they ate in silence, then with a dog-like look of devotion she asked guiltily, "What sort of case?"

"Murder."

"God! Isn't that dangerous?"

"It's terrific. Perks, promotion, pay increase . . ."

"Who's been murdered?"

"Don't know. Only heard this evening. I'm getting the file tomorrow . . ."

Looking at him with a mixture of love and pity, she wondered how anyone so weak, insignificant yet adorable, could possibly be given a real murder to investigate. Film sleuths were always tough, boozy, beefy.

"Put the kettle on while I feed her," she said, as Yana's wailing penetrated from the living room.

"How many cases have you got?" Major Leonid Ivanovich Ratko, known affectionately as Ratty, asked Viktor next morning.

"Twenty-seven."

"Anything serious?"

"Seven lift muggings, four flat burglaries, one trading-stall arson. The rest's small stuff."

"Five Militia Academy cadets arrive tomorrow, so you pass that lot to them, having selected one to assist you."

A major still at fifty, a major Ratko would remain till the day he died, being of those who give not a damn for their futures, and vaunt as much in scruffiness and scant use of the razor. Whether promotion to lieutenant colonel would have reformed him was hard to say. The odds were against it. At Ratko's age old habits died hard.

"Here's the file, have a look, then come back," he said wearily, indicating the door.

Back in his tiny office with its cracked and draughty window, Viktor eyed the two vacant desks opposite. The occupant of one was under investigation and not likely to return; the other was away on detachment. Peace and quiet, then, in which to concentrate.

First came photographs of a corpse whose neck bore the telltale marks of hanging, and as he proceeded to read he remembered his pal Dima Rakin, now of Special Branch F., who had looked in yesterday to see Ratko, saying something about a retired general taking a fatal balloon flight.

"Get the picture?" asked Ratko, having knocked and entered.

"Not yet, Chief."

Taking a chair from one of the other desks, Ratko sat opposite Viktor.

"Any questions?"

"I've not read to the end."

"None so far, then. Well, that's odd, because I've got some."

"For me?"

"For whoever kicked this one our way . . . Got a kettle? Make tea, and we'll talk."

But it was the Major who talked, eyes fixed on Viktor.

"One: it's too fresh a case to write off as a dead ender. Two: seeing it's a Government corpse, it's logically a job for some big nob and a whole team of investigators. But no, we get it. Our patch was where he took off from, so OK, regardless of where he came down. Nothing in the papers. No obituary. So there's a clamp-down."

Viktor nodded agreement.

"Why the order to give you the case?"

"Me?"

"You personally, the chap on the phone said . . . So we've got connections, have we? But they're what you need to keep clear of this sort of thing."

"Maybe Dima's something to do with it. He's always popping in."

"He's your pal – ask him. At least find out how best to tackle it. Right, I've sat here long enough. Read to the end, then come and see me."

Viktor was alone again, fanciful ideas as to the whys and wherefores of being assigned the ballooning general cruelly shattered. His mood was now one of gloom. Disinclined to read, he spread the photographs on the desk, leant back, and gazed out at a grey, diagonally cracked glass rectangle of city.

4

Awakening to the caress of warm sunlight on his face, Nik might have been back in Granny's little chalet near Zhitomir, where his bed was under a window.

He showered, shaved, and investigating the fridge, found it thoughtfully stocked with cheese, sausage, vegetables, and three eggs, enough for a decent omelette.

He wondered how Tanya and Volodya were getting on and what they were eating. He'd left them a thousand of the six thousand dollars he'd received for the flat, telling them to go easy, as they'd need money for here.

After breakfast he dressed, went out, and walked until he came to a gate, at which a soldier was asleep on a chair. He was unarmed. Ukraine, in contrast to Tadzhikistan, was a land at peace. He'd done well to come.

Exploring further, Nik found himself looking down on a meandering willow-bordered river with ducks. He went down some steps to where there were boats moored, then followed the towpath, revelling in the keen morning air.

"Any luck?" he asked quietly, coming upon a fisherman.

"Some, but it's slow work."

Feeling a need to talk, Nik inquired if he was from these parts.

"I live just up there. You on holiday?"

"Since yesterday. Are there any shops?"

"You've got a food store on site, and there's a couple of shops in Koncha-Zaspa, twenty minutes from here. You're not from Kiev then?"

"Tadzhikistan. Left my family in Saratov, and come on ahead to find a flat. What are prices like?"

"In Kiev, upwards of ten thousand dollars for a one-roomer."

Nik was aghast.

"Against six thousand dollars for a three-roomer in Dushanbe . . ."

The fisherman looked sympathetic.

"You didn't check beforehand?"

Nik said nothing, suddenly remembering that he'd no local currency, just the dollars for the flat, and must ask Ivan Lvovich about the promised removal expenses.

"As the fish are no longer biting, how about coffee at my place?" said the fisherman.

Nik watched him reel in, but his thoughts were elsewhere. The idea of cheap accommodation had been central to his plans for their future in a new country, and here was a complete stranger upsetting all that and inviting him to coffee.

"Not to worry, affordable," had been Ivan Lvovich's response when he'd asked about prices. Affordable, but not to him.

"You coming?" the fisherman inquired, standing with his rod and a can containing his catch.

"Thanks, I'd like to."

They went up a steep track, through a gate, and on past a massive, old two-storey house.

"My mother-in-law's place," said the fisherman. "And that," indicating the fine three-storeyed brick-built house ahead of them, "is what I built. With help from my son and some locals."

9

"So you're a builder."

"Writer. It's a writers' colony here. Like Peredelkino outside Moscow."

The entrance led straight into a vast kitchen. A long pine table stood before a long, old-fashioned high-backed leather sofa.

Nik ran his hand over the table's polished surface.

"Made that too," said the fisherman over his shoulder, lighting the stove, and setting the coffee mill whirring.

At that moment a woman in only a nightdress started down the stairs, went back, then reappeared, now wearing a housecoat.

"Svetlana, my wife," said the fisherman. "I'm Valentin."

"I'm Nik."

"I asked Nik back for coffee," Valentin explained. "He's from Dushanbe."

"I'll have some too," said Svetlana. She was tall, graceful, wide-eyed and vaguely aristocratic, very different from Nik's earthy, countrified Tanya.

"We were late to bed," Valentin explained. "We had friends from Kiev and sat up drinking till two. Which always means I wake at five, and there's nothing for it but to go fishing."

"Caught anything?" Svetlana asked.

"Seven roach."

5

Nik found an agitated Ivan Lvovich waiting outside the chalet.

"Thought something had happened," he complained. "You couldn't possibly have slept through my knocking!"

"Back in a day or two, you said." Nik reminded him, getting out the key.

"Yes, but situations can change, and fast. You go and sit down, I'll put on the kettle."

Nik dutifully went and sat down in the sitting room.

"Found a bug behind my kitchen radiator," Ivan Lvovich continued, joining him. "Someone's digging. You haven't, I trust, been fraternizing with the natives."

"No," Nik lied.

"See that you don't. Things are moving, and we must get our skates on. No more recuperating."

He went to attend to the kettle, and when he returned with the tea his hands were shaking slightly.

"To be honest, we had not intended to brief you straightaway," he said. "At least, not fully. Now we must. Our former KGB is facing reforms which aren't to some people's liking. But what matters is, that *we* have the President's go-ahead.

"Top priority is the setting up of a Ukrainian Federal Bureau along the lines of the FBI. What's needed are two services in place of the one, so as to ensure greater control over the loyalty and accountability to the government of both.

"Official moves in this direction have been killed off by Parliament. Not to their advantage, they say. Heads would roll. You see, at present, Ukrainian Security has the monopoly of incriminating evidence to exploit as it sees fit, regarding its interests as identical with the State's. But a monopoly shared is a monopoly impaired – hence the antagonism.

"So what's the problem?" Ivan Lvovich continued. "Simply that we do not have the funds for setting up a Federal Bureau. Funny, if it weren't so serious! I'm Security old style. What I see being recruited nowadays is garbage. Straight in off the street. No principles. Out, at best, to make a career; at worst, to use Security for cover. Our Federal Bureau, when achieved, will be to Ukrainian Security what the KGB once was to the militia – more above board, and dedicated to the State's interests. Would, I ask you, anyone in the old days have got away with trying to kill the Prime Minister? Or gunning down a deputy at the airport and calmly driving off?"

Raising his cup to his lips, he blew on it before taking a gulp.

11

"All this goes no further, and for reasons other than your being duty-bound to secrecy. It's bigger than us. It's dangerous, potentially fatal, stuff. It's State's interests *über alles* now, human frailty included. Sentimentality, emotion, they're out. Absolute devotion to duty, instant, unswerving obedience, they're what's needed. As in any security service.

"As to funding: Russia, as you're probably aware, has appropriated all Soviet property abroad, acting as self-styled *lawful heir of the Great and Indivisible*. But that other *Great and Indivisible*, the KGB, was possessed of even more property and investments abroad which have never been heard about. KGB colleagues of mine from former Soviet republics tried to raise the matter officially. I didn't even make it to their funerals. I was advised against going. It's a delicate subject which no-one at State level will touch, even though Ukrainian Security's fair share of the proceeds is conservatively estimated at not less than a billion dollars.

"In the main, it's *active* property: banks, businesses, factories, hotels – at least one in Switzerland – all operationally financed originally, and thereafter generating income, even spawning independent operations. One per cent of that lot would put us in business.

"Still, enough for today. Chew it over. Relaxing's done with. You've work to do."

"What?" Nik asked.

"Tell you later. That all?"

"How about a flat? And when my family joins me?"

"The flat will have to wait. Something decent's what you want, and your present funds don't run to it."

"There'd be something *affordable*, you said!"

"To the Federal Bureau, yes, when funds materialize and we're up and running. Meanwhile, you've got this place free."

"How about our container?"

"No sweat. That'll hole up in some customs warehouse, and

12

we'll pay storage. But put your feet up, have a think. I'm going for a stroll."

The ensuing silence seemed cheerless, alarming. His future was veiled in obscurity.

The prospect of work held no terrors. Indeed, the degree of trust implicit in the Colonel's proposal was flattering and a plus. As also the Colonel's chancing to select him just when he was doing his damnedest to get out of Tadzhikistan. His one anxiety was the prospect of extended separation from Tanya and Volodya. He wondered how they were, how they were eating, what they were doing.

Lying back on the sofa, he closed his eyes. What better than to spend his coming fortieth birthday with Tanya and Volodya? He could fly to Saratov. It would be a month or so before he found a flat.

6

Viktor bumped into Dima Rakin unexpectedly, while taking a breath of fresh air.

"Out and about in working hours?" Dima challenged.

"Looking for you, as a matter of fact."

"A likely tale."

"No, seriously."

"Let's go somewhere and sit down."

The Grey Tom basement bar was empty, and Dima had to rap the counter with a coin before a girl appeared.

The marble table top was icy to the touch, and after the sun outside the bar seemed distinctly chilly.

"Tell me all," said Dima.

"As I expect you know, I've got a murder case."

"Your big chance. Well done!"

"Not so sure."

Dima affected surprise.

"It feels like a setup. Petty crime's what I deal with. Not murdered Presidential Advisers!"

"Is that you speaking, or Ratko?"

"What's the difference?"

Dima pulled a pack of cigarettes from his shirt pocket and lit one.

"It was me suggested you," he said quietly between puffs. "I'll explain, so far as I can, but it doesn't amount to much, if I'm honest."

He crushed the partially smoked cigarette into the ashtray.

Viktor got himself another coffee, and for some minutes they sat in silence. Dima crushed out a second cigarette.

"I thought you'd be good at the incidental lines of inquiry."

"Such as?"

"External pressure, involvements, anonymous tip-offs . . . the normal stuff. Nothing to worry about. Make a good job of it and you could find yourself in a nice warm office with a proper window . . . Read the file? Well, what are you waiting for? Get marching, singing as you go! Like in the army!"

"*Can* a good job be made of it?"

Dima grinned ruefully.

"Depends . . . But don't worry, you won't be out in the cold. Help and advice will be forthcoming. You'll see. And I'm there on the phone."

He gave Viktor his card.

After the subterranean bar, the sunny side of the street was doubly pleasant.

Ratko greeted him with a knowing wink.

"Phone call from the Ministry. You're big time, it seems. I'll have to watch my step."

"Balls! Big-time luck is what I need."

"Anyway, you won't get brained by a brick – you've got wheels.

Or will have within the hour. A Mazda, one of ten, gift to the MVD from the Ukrainian Transport Bank! Democracy in action. Quite right, too. Better than two per general! What news from his nibs? Or were you just taking a breather?"

"What Dima said was – "

"Don't want to know. You're the blue-eyed boy. I've got an officeful of cadets. Come and feast your eyes."

The five skinny, lookalike young cadets in militia uniform were, like most of their generation, pale, pimply, wary.

"All keen to get cracking, eh?" demanded the Major.

The "Yes, Major!" was unenthusiastic and not in unison.

"Lieutenant Slutsky, here," he continued, giving Viktor a grin, "will now address you and give you your case files. After which, all questions to me. Stupid questions will forfeit rations. OK?"

Exit Ratko, grinning.

"I'll fetch your files," said Viktor before darting out after him.

"Address them? What about?"

"Got to be an address. It says so in regs. And it's not for an old cynic like me to witter on about honesty, probity, duty . . . Shoot 'em the odd slogan, bung 'em their case files, and pick an assistant. He can brew your coffee, fetch beer, but that's about the best you can expect."

He spoke for three minutes – the limit of their attention span – and as he gave out files, noted down names: Polishchuk, Petrov, Plachinda, Kovinko, Zanozin.

"Any questions?"

"The waiting list for a flat, how to get on it?" one asked, clearly speaking for all.

"Question for the Major," Viktor said calmly. "All been assigned offices?"

"One between the lot of us," someone said.

"To your office then!"

He went over to the window. From first-floor level the city looked surprisingly green and peaceful. Kids playing, as if it were high summer.

"Picked your man?" Ratko asked from the door.

"Not yet. I haven't seen enough of them."

"I've grabbed your spare desks . . . Post mortem findings due twenty minutes from now, so don't go sloping off."

"Post mortem?"

"Even dead generals have to have one. And now, having warmed my office, do the same to your own."

Returning to the file and photographs, Viktor read:

Bronitsky, Vadim Aleksandrovich, b. Kresty, Donyetsk Region, m., one son. Address: Kiev, Suvorov St, 26, Flat 133.

Surprisingly, there was no mention of service or place of employment, and while Viktor pondered the fact, gazing at sunlit foliage seen through cracked glass, the phone rang.

"Come."

With Ratko was a man in civilian clothes. He handed Viktor keys and a plastic folder of vehicle documents, and advised taking it easily at first, as he'd find the Mazda livelier than the Zaporozhets.

"Nose back to grindstone then," said Radko when the man had gone. "Show ourselves deserving of the high trust reposed in us."

The day was drawing in. Viktor made tea, then tackled the post-mortem report. *Death from cardiac arrest* ran the verdict. He shrugged. In which case Murder was out, and Malicious Hooliganism or Desecration of the Dead was in.

Odd, though, to get strung by the neck to a balloon when dead, and sent skywards.

The address and telephone number of the forensic laboratory were as legible as the pathologist's signature was not.

Now at 7.30 no-one would be there. Gathering everything into the file, he picked up the car keys.

"You've got remote locking," volunteered the sergeant on guard approvingly, and taking the key from him, demonstrated what could be done.

Viktor drove slowly and cautiously, incurring derisive hoots from similarly fast and flashy cars.

He was half way over Southern Bridge, when a mobile phone warbled in the dashboard recess.

"Like it?" a man's voice inquired.

"Very much! But who's that?"

"Georgiy Georgievich. I'll be your sidekick – like in American cop films."

"When?" asked Viktor, mystified.

"As of right now. You're no longer solo, so get used to it. It'll be easier that way, and safer. Happy?"

"Not entirely."

"Make a note of my mobile number: 240-80-90. Having seen the postmortem report, shouldn't you have a word with the pathologist?"

"I'm going to."

"Good man! Don't leave your mobile in the car!"

As he drew up outside their block, his spirits plunged. Once again he'd forgotten to collect their ration entitlement.

Having pocketed his phone and locked by remote control, he still checked all four doors and the boot, before looking round for any likely car thieves. But apart from lonely figures on the track between blocks and metro, there was no one about.

7

Ivan Lvovich returned later than expected, having met someone in a bar.

News of a bar in the vicinity prompted Nik to raise the question of money.

"Of course. I forgot."

Reaching into an inner pocket, Ivan Lvovich produced an envelope.

"Something to be going on with, and why not adjourn to the bar.

Drinks on me. Just one thing, though, before we go. If you're not happy, Nik, about what I've said so far, you can back out, go to Saratov, live your own life, so long as you remain bound to secrecy."

"I'm quite happy," Nik responded, putting on his jacket.

Ivan Lvovich smiled.

"Come on, let's go."

Ivan Lvovich ordered, and they sat out on the terrace overlooking the river. The air was fresh and invigorating. He would come back here on his own, Nik decided. It was a pleasant spot.

"To our joint success!" said Ivan Lvovich raising his squat tumbler of vodka.

Nik downed his in a gulp, before noticing that Ivan Lvovich had merely sipped his.

"I'll get you another."

A young couple came and stood gazing down at the full moon reflected in the river.

"You must bring your wife here," Ivan Lvovich was saying when his mobile rang.

"Fine," he said, with the phone to his ear. "It's now 21.45 . . . Understood."

Popping a slice of lemon into his mouth and his mobile into his pocket, he took another sip of vodka.

"Things are warming up," he said wearily. "But no rush. We've half an hour before we go into town."

"For what?" Nik asked, only to receive a disapproving look.

Taking another slice of lemon, Ivan Lvovich consulted his watch.

"Like films?" he asked, his friendly self again.

"Why?"

"You'll see."

8

Shooting lights at amber, sometimes at red, the dark blue BMW sped through the deserted streets of Kiev to a backstreet in Podol.

Ordering his driver to wait, Ivan Lvovich hustled Nik along to where, around the corner, a minivan bearing the legend "Miller Ltd Suspended Ceilings" was parked. The driver opened the rear doors, and they climbed into something resembling a tiny television studio.

Ivan Lvovich passed Nik a collapsible stool.

"Sit and watch."

One monitor showed a corridor with coat pegs and a mirror; another, a kitchen with a round table, an enormous refrigerator and refinements seen only in such few Western magazines as reached Dushanbe. A third showed a middle-aged man bound to a rocking chair. On the corridor monitor a door – probably the bathroom – opened and a man in jeans and a T-shirt came out carrying a shoulder bag, looked at himself in the mirror, smiled, and passing out of camera view, reappeared in the room with the rocking-chair. From his bag he took an audio cassette which he inserted in a radio cassette recorder.

Ivan Lvovich called for sound.

"Coming," said the young man at the control-panel.

"Can you get it louder?"

Background hiss broken by rhythmical beats, then, from the prisoner, a feeble "That was nothing to do with me! Nothing! I've been framed!"

"Can happen to the best," said the other man, squatting and taking from his bag an object dangling wires. These he connected to some other device, and after consulting his watch, placed both objects beneath the rocking-chair.

"Like it louder?"

The beat became deafening.

"What is it?" Nik asked.

"Human heart."

The man was now in the kitchen, taking sausage from the fridge, after which he cut bread and made coffee.

The prisoner meanwhile was rocking to and fro in a vain effort to free himself.

"Don't we get any coffee?" asked Ivan Lvovich.

The young engineer produced a thermos. Ivan Lvovich poured, drank, then poured for Nik.

"Enjoying it?"

Bewildered, Nik shrugged.

"Take a good look at that chap. That's Sergey Vladimirovich Sakhno. Age thirty-three. Interesting type. Eventful life. Ex-sapper officer. Invalided out following death of his pregnant girlfriend. Psychologically dodgy. His prisoner had some involvement in the death of the girl. It's the unborn baby's heartbeat we're hearing, courtesy of ultrasound scan. In my day a lock of hair in an envelope was sufficient. The new technology caters for any madness. – But hang on!"

After a last look at the prisoner, Sakhno was on his way out, half-eaten sandwich abandoned on the table.

"Can't we go and defuse the damned thing?"

"No point."

"He'll be killed, for God's sake!"

"Yes, because we're not supposed to be here. The people who have brought this about are watching from a similar vehicle on the other side of the block. This isn't our scene, and it's time to be going."

At a gesture from him the monitors dimmed, and hiss and heartbeats gave way to an uneasy silence that was in contrast to Nik's inner turmoil.

"Did that have to happen?" he asked, as they sped back through the sleeping city.

"He was framed, like he said, but didn't actually kill the girl. He was due to die for other reasons. Sakhno's carried out the sentence. Why I said take a good look is because you're shortly to meet and become friends. To which end, tomorrow evening you make a promising start by saving his life."

"A stage-managed rescue?"

"No, for real. With this one-off assignment, Sakhno becomes disposable. And disposability is not something I go for. The same applies to plastic forks, spoons and paper plates."

"So I save his life, then what?"

"Your work really starts. You get him away, lie low, then move on. Keeping yourself out of the picture, that's the main thing. So long as you stay an unknown quantity, you're safe."

They travelled on in silence through a cold, lifeless, indifferent city, through villages and the familiar forest.

"Sleep till eleven," advised Ivan Lvovich as they parted.

9

Viktor sat in his kitchen with the light off and moon enough to locate his teacup by.

2.30 a.m. Not a sound, beyond the tick of the wall clock. Wife, daughter, city were asleep.

He had, thanks to Reutmann, the pathologist, learnt a little more concerning General Bronitsky. Death had occurred lateish on May 20th, Bronitsky having dined well and drunk spirits. The stomach contents: partially digested cured fillet of sturgeon, salami, red caviar pancakes, suggested hurried consumption. The rope had been attached after death, the cause of which, at variance with the clean bill of health awarded by the General's medical board on retirement, was a massive coronary thrombosis. Aged forty-seven, he had not been a heavy drinker, and enjoyed canoeing and hunting.

Viktor next visited Bronitsky's widow, with whom he sat and talked in homely fashion in the kitchen. Emotions well under control, she poured cognac and they drank to her husband's memory. A source of grievance was the failure to release his body for burial, and Viktor promised to hurry things up.

She answered his questions calmly, matter-of-factly.

Her husband had no real friends. At Staff HQ he had had any number, but not since becoming Adviser. Apple of his eye was son Boris, now studying in England. He, as it happened, had left by air two days before his father's death, and would thus be spared being questioned and the pain of the funeral. He was only eighteen. His fees were paid, but only for the first six months, which had been a worry, until colleagues of her husband promised State funding for a year, after which he could complete his studies in Ukraine.

Recalling this in the still of the Kiev night, Viktor thought of at least five more questions he ought to have asked. Helpful as they'd seemed at the time, her ramblings did not, he now saw, contribute anything of consequence.

Tiptoeing to the living-room balcony, he made sure that his Mazda was still safe.

Returning to the kitchen and punching two holes in a tin of ration-entitlement condensed milk, he drank, helping it down with cold tea.

Outside in the corridor his mobile rang in the pocket of his jacket, and in three strides he reached and answered it.

"Me, Georgiy. Hi!"

"Hi," said Viktor, taken aback.

"Couldn't sleep, thought I'd ring. Seen the widow?"

"Yes."

"Learn anything?"

"Next to nothing."

"That's because she was on her home ground. Get her out to a café earlyish, when she's got herself in order but not her thoughts.

As in football, it's harder to win away. Get it?"

"I think so."

"You ring her tomorrow at ten, tell her you'll pick her up at eleven and put the phone down. You must be a fellow insomniac . . . Speak to you later."

From the window Viktor saw headlights go on, then move slowly away along the metro road.

"You look like death warmed up!" said Ira over breakfast next morning.

"Don't worry, I'll catch up on sleep," he said, largely to himself, as Ira hurried away to feed their crying daughter.

He breakfasted in solitude, then went to the balcony to check on his car.

Strung out along the road, like Napoleon's army retreating to Smolensk, an ant-like safari of commuters was making for the metro.

For a while he sat in the bedroom, where Ira was feeding Yana, but feeling superfluous, soon returned to the kitchen. At 9.30, when the metro road was deserted, except for kids with toy tommy guns playing "New Russians", he rang Bronitsky's widow, as suggested.

Widow Bronitsky in long black skirt and emerald blouse was sitting outside her residence when Viktor drove up and dutifully opened the door.

"So much for the myth of militia poverty!" she said, impressed by the car.

The Grey Tom bar, steps still wet from washing, was only just open and apart from the bar girl, deserted.

He settled the widow at the corner table where he and Dima had sat.

"Coffee?"

"And cognac."

Georgiy was right. Calmly, casually, smiling, mildly flirtatious in her melancholy, she came up with real answers. The lost friends had, in fact, departed the scene after scandal over a leak. There was hell to pay, a major clampdown. A colonel committed suicide, a female civilian secretary disappeared, and three senior HQ staff turned up in Moscow in cosy flats on Kutuzov Prospekt, and were duly followed by their families. Maksim Ivin, who was one of them, had phoned several times since. He'd been her husband's best friend in the old days and a constant visitor. He and her husband hunted together, and played *préférence*.

"Don't you need three for that?" Viktor objected.

"Maksim would call his son or some subordinate over, and they'd play on long after I'd gone to bed. Next morning there'd be one of them on the sofa, another in a chair."

They talked on over coffee and cognac, but as the morning advanced and the cognac took effect, the Widow Bronitsky said progressively less and the intervals between question and answer lengthened. Viktor decided to call it a day.

"Don't forget what you said about getting the body released," she reminded him. "It's so awkward. Colleagues, neighbours all the time phoning and asking when the funeral is."

Viktor said he'd not forgotten.

He drove her to her door and was rewarded with a pleasant smile.

He returned to District shortly before one only to learn that Bronitsky's body was missing, the antediluvian alarm at the forensic lab. having been deactivated during the night. Pausing only to jot down the salient points of his interview, Viktor dashed out to his car.

10

Not having drawn his curtain, Nik woke with the sun at 5.15. How long had he slept? Two hours? Three? He had no idea.

Things were moving fast. How and where he was to rescue Sakhno, he had yet to discover. But soon they'd be on the run. So what to do with his things? And the five thousand dollars wrapped in a towel in his case?

Ivan Lvovich was coming at 11.00. It was now only 5.30. He had time, but for what?

Mechanically, he got up, dressed, put the kettle on, sliced bread, sausage, cheese, drank coffee, and began to think more calmly.

He couldn't take his cases with him, and wasn't keen on leaving them in the chalet. He could have left them with friends, but his having no friends in Kiev or anywhere else in Ukraine was why he was here, ideally unidentifiable if found dead, even if pictured on television. Provided Valentin and Svetlana weren't watching . . . Now there was a thought!

Leaving his coffee, he dragged both cases from under the bed and took out the towel-wrapped dollars, a notebook, and a folder containing birth certificate, army papers, marriage certificate.

It would be nice to give them something. The Phillips electric razor, bought on stupid impulse, still boxed and unused, instructions in Arabic – as if one needed to be told how to shave! – would do for Valentin. And for Svetlana, the fine Chinese fountain pen with which he wrote the address of their Saratov relatives. With dollars, papers and presents in a Marlboro carrier bag, he set off. All was quiet.

Valentin was not, as he had hoped, fishing.

The house, when he reached it, was sleeping. He hesitated to knock, but in the end he did. There was nothing else for it.

The sleepy Valentin who eventually opened he greeted with a torrent of apology.

"Bit off colour, I'm afraid," Valentin confessed, letting him in. "Either a cold or something I ate. Like some tea?"

Seated again at the long pine table, Nik produced his presents.

"I have a favour to ask – that is, if you've not said anything to anyone about our having met."

"I haven't, no," said Valentin, clearly surprised.

"And don't, please. I've been called away. I can't say more. And since you are the only people I know here, I'd like to leave these things."

He emptied the carrier on the table.

"Money, papers, my wife's address. If I'm not back in two months, let her know you have my stuff . . . I'm sorry to land you with this."

"No problem."

Returning to the chalet, Nik made a second breakfast, then sat outside on the wooden step.

Sun, birds, trees – a fairy-tale morning! Such as he wished all his mornings to be!

A woodpecker began to hammer. Eventually he spotted it high up on a tall dead pine. The first he'd heard since childhood. There'd been no woodpeckers in Tadzhikistan.

11

So far Viktor had worked solo, with no one, apart from the invisible Georgiy, showing any interest in the case of the retired general, though the Mazda and mobile phone were evidence of its importance to someone somewhere.

The disappearance of the body brought about a change: phone calls from Directorate, phone calls from Ministry, both demanding an all-out effort.

Even Ratko was involved, to the extent of switching Viktor's cadets onto the search for the corpse, though to what effect, with them taking their ease in some café, it was hard to imagine.

Viktor was dozing at his desk when Georgiy rang.

"Six bodies so far, in case you haven't heard."

"One of them Bronitsky's?"

"Could be. I'm waiting to hear – they're all in different morgues – but I doubt it. No sense in pinching a body, then dumping it where even the militia can find it. These will just be the homeless or suicides. And by the way, it's not just militia on the job."

"Security?"

"Not them, though they do, it's true, 'render emergency assistance' . . . No, military counterintelligence. Sit back, quiet as mice, then pop out like like ants in the spring."

"He was, after all, General Staff."

"Then Defence Adviser to the President. And don't you think it a bit odd, retiring, then going on being involved?"

"No."

"Well, sleep on it," said Georgiy amiably, ringing off.

Viktor informed Ratko of the six bodies, but two hours later the search was resumed. Georgiy had been right.

It was nearly 10.00 before Viktor arrived home, exhausted and convinced there would be no new developments till morning.

Ira and Yana were in bed.

Throwing himself onto the living-room sofa, he fell instantly asleep.

Three hours later his mobile rang and continued to ring until retrieved from his jacket hung over a chair.

"Still awake?" asked the familiar voice.

"Actually no."

"You should be. Time to get moving."

"Now? Where?"

"Just heard from an obliging smuggler: would we kindly relieve him and his aircraft of a neatly packaged corpse."

"What aircraft?"

"You really are awake?"

"Yes."

"Then listen. Thirty minutes from now you set off for Zhulyany Airport. Just beyond the Sevastopol Square roundabout, you stop, flash your warning lights for a minute, then drive on. You'll be overtaken by two vehicles, a Volga and a minivan. The snatch squad. They've got their orders. To the right of the terminal building there's a gate onto the airfield. It'll be open. Drive out to the AN-26, where you'll see the snatch squad parked. The plane takes off at 0300 hrs. You disembark the body, but touch nothing on board. Silence essential – don't use your horn. We don't want customs and the like in on the scene."

The terminal concourse beneath its blue neon KIEV ZHULYANY was as brightly illuminated as the city streets were not.

Cutting his lights, Viktor drove a little way onto an apron of sleeping aircraft, lowered his window and breathed in the keen night air. His watch showed 02.15. The only sounds were the rustle of grass and the faint drumming of some insect.

Way out on the airfield, headlights flashed on and off, and Viktor drove in their direction, now over concrete, now over grass, avoiding the landing lights and stubby striped marker posts.

Two masked Special Forces men armed with short Kalashnikovs were standing guard by the loading doors of an AN-26 of Belarusian Airlines. One motioned him to climb aboard. Two others were stationed at the tail where the Volga and the minivan were parked.

At the top of the ramp he was greeted by an officer, also masked, who led him towards the rear between strapped-down loads and carefully stowed cartons, crates and canvas trunks.

"Here we are," he said, indicating a zipped up canvas bag at the end of the aisle.

A Special Forces man drew down the zip a little, and his powerful torch showed a man's face under milky polythene. The air was heavy with a sour, pungent odour. He zipped the bag up again.

28

"Is it him?" Viktor asked the officer.

"We'll know in an hour. But let's get out of here. Hazardous cargo."

The odour was now overpowering.

"Chemicals?" Viktor asked.

"Apart from the liquid nitrogen in the body bag, no. More the province of nuclear physics."

They quickly left the plane, followed by two men carrying the body bag which they loaded into the minivan.

"Where was the body going?"

"Russia. Voronezh."

"I'd have thought Moscow, where his friends are."

The eyes in the mask shot him an odd look.

"Isn't Russia one big Moscow?"

Standing under a wing out of earshot, Viktor phoned Georgiy.

Georgiy told him he should now go home and get some sleep. He would ring in the morning.

As he got into his car, Viktor saw three scared-looking aircrew emerge from the Volga and scuttle up the ramp into their plane.

Half dead with fatigue, he drove, slumped forward onto the wheel, eyes fixed on the deserted road ahead. What had been the sense of his being there? Special Forces had managed perfectly without him. His only answer was the road in the Mazda's headlights.

12

Ivan Lvovich turned up at 10.55, made himself a cheese sandwich, and as he ate and Nik drank coffee, talked.

"One," he began, "whatever the situation, keep calm, don't fly off the handle. Act slow-witted. Gives you time to think . . .

"Two, no playing the smart-arse with Sakhno. Treat him like

29

your kid brother. If he gets het up, go easy. You're his rescuer, and he must trust you as such – that's essential.

"Tonight you and he travel to Sarny, Belarus. The tickets are on their way. You spend the night in the hotel outside the station, and tomorrow you take the 13.00 bus to Brest. In Brest you overnight in a hotel, get tourist vouchers for Poland, and proceed to Poznan, where, you tell him, you've a good friend who can fix things. Alex Wozniak's your friend. Telephone 555-421. Ex-Security. At some point, out of Sakhno's hearing, he'll brief you further."

He produced an American Express card.

"Seen one of these?"

"Only in films."

"But you've got the idea. I'll give you a thousand dollars in notes to see you through the first few days. Spend sensibly. From Poland on, you can use the card for tickets and hotels. But no lashing out. Sign your name on the back."

"My real name?"

"So long as it's illegible. And against his perhaps becoming a menace, you'd better have these by you." He handed Nik eight tablets embedded in plastic. "One – in tea, coffee or beer – is the dose."

He got to his feet.

"This evening we eat here. I'll bring the food. You stay in. If you need fresh air, open a window. If you're bored, look at the papers."

"What papers?"

"Try the letter box. And always, Nik, before relaxing, be vigilant of your surroundings. Keep your wits about you."

The letter box yielded copies of Kiev News, All-Ukraine Gazette and Voice of Ukraine.

CORPSE ON SECURITY ROOF, he read, INVESTIGATION STALEMATE, before turning the page in search of the crossword.

As he reached for his pen, he thought suddenly of Ivan Lvovich's advice on the score of vigilance, and checked for hidden cameras. But apart from a white box no larger than a cigarette pack in a corner of the hall ceiling, left of the sitting-room door – probably a smoke detector – he found nothing.

Throwing open the window, he sat and thought of Tanya and Volodya now daily expecting a telegram saying they were to join him. He must tell them about the hold-up. There must be a post or telegraph office. Except that he'd been told to stay in. But which was the more important: contact his wife or obey an old man who, so far, had not kept a single promise of his own?

It might not be too late to leave a letter or wording for a telegram with Valentin. Preferably a telegram. And some money.

AT LEAST MONTH DELAY, he wrote on a scrap of paper, DONT WORRY LOVE YOU MISS YOU NIK.

But as he opened the door to go in search of a post office, there was Ivan Lvovich's driver standing beside his dark blue BMW and staring hard.

Why not simply get Ivan Lvovich to send it? Adding the address in Saratov, he slipped the scrap of paper into his pocket, and returned to the papers. Mad and unreal as it seemed, there really had been a corpse on the roof of State Security. Why, no one could say. Prosecutor's Office and State Security were refusing to comment since investigations were ongoing, as also the President's Office, where the dead man had been employed.

Ivan Lvovich arrived with two carrier bags.

"Quick: knives, forks, before it gets cold!" he ordered, unloading meat and fish hors d'oeuvre, salad and vegetables, and by the time Nik brought them, plates of chips and giant pork chops were ready on the table.

"And some glasses!" he added, opening a bottle of Akhasheni.

They drank, as on the first evening, to success, then enjoyed their meal in silence.

After a second glass of the excellent Georgian wine, Nik asked Ivan Lvovich if he would send a telegram for him.

"Of course! And as I've got my camera we could send her a photo."

He took two shots of Nik, then, using the shutter-timer, one of him and Nik together, for himself.

13

Viktor's day began earlier than expected. Georgiy rang at 8.30, giving him twenty minutes to shower and breakfast.

No sooner had he put the kettle on and two eggs to boil, than Georgiy rang back.

"Got something to write with? One: find out from Widow B. where and in whose company her husband spent his last few days, May 20th especially. Two: has she informed their Moscow pals of his death? If so, get their phone numbers. Three: send a cadet to collect restaurant menus for the 20th. But why tell you your job! Who's investigating? You or me?"

The sudden show of irritation was as surprising as it was off-putting.

"You, I'd say."

"You would, would you? And wouldn't you also say that *you* should get organized?"

Georgiy was right. He had yet to set out and analyse what he'd learnt concerning Bronitsky. Still, he'd not been at it all that long.

"Understood," said Viktor.

"Good man. Now, some news for you. It *was* Bronitsky's body you foiled the illegal export of. So the widow can go ahead with arrangements. They'll release the body tomorrow, especially now there's a luxury coffin with bronze handles which his colleagues clubbed together for. And another thing – and not your problem – those who lay him out will have to put left hand over right."

"How so?"

"Someone's sliced his right thumb off as a keepsake."

"What the hell for?"

"Who's doing the investigating?"

"Me. But knowing who you are would help."

"Tough, talking to an abstraction, eh?" The voice softened. "Well, here's the picture: age, forty-five; height 182; hair short, dark; bachelor; whisky-on-the-rocks man; non-smoker; jogs five kilometres daily. That do?"

"Not quite what I had in mind."

"I know."

"Am I allowed another question?"

"Go ahead."

"Why the airport trip? Special Forces had it all buttoned up."

"To show them who was in charge, and now they've seen you, they know. I'll never ask you to do anything that doesn't make sense. Sense there will be, if not apparent. How are we feeling?"

"Fine."

"So ring the widow and arrange to meet as soon as possible."

From that point on, the day went as smoothly as a train downhill. Delighted at the release of her husband's body, Widow Bronitsky talked for half an hour, yielding more than he'd bargained for. He duly noted the address and phone number of Maksim Ivin, as well as the phone numbers of Bronitsky's two pals now in Moscow. The son had gone off to his Cambridge language school without saying goodbye. He'd had a major row with his father, but had been driven by his father's chauffeur to the airport. Ivin had visited Kiev two days before her husband's death. He'd not come to the house but stayed at a hotel. He must have met up with her husband at least once, because her husband had brought her a gift of Yves St Laurent perfume from him.

All this Viktor wrote up before lunch, copying addresses and phone numbers from crumpled scraps of paper, then called the smartest-looking of the cadets to his office, and sent him to chase up menus for May 20th.

"How do I know what restaurants there are?"

"Get the Major's *Kiev A to Z*, make a list and tick them off. Red caviar pancakes are what you're after. Make a good job of it, and you can assist further with the investigation."

The cadet brightened.

"And you are?"

"Zanozin, Mikhail."

"Report back every three hours. If I'm out, leave a note."

Taking a sheet of paper, Viktor listed, on the left, friends and relatives seen by Bronitsky shortly before his death, and on the right, who to interview: former colleagues, those he played cards and hunted with, and the son in England.

The son would probably come back for the funeral. So, too, the Moscow friends, who had phoned and asked about arrangements.

Writing *Corpse | Zhulyany – Voronezh | thumb?* on his sheet of paper, he wondered about this obliging smuggler of Georgiy's who had surrendered the body to avoid being incriminated. Or was he thick with Georgiy and dependent on him for his AN-26 charter flights? Either way, he'd been of assistance, and suitably rewarded, no doubt. As to the thumb, well . . . More important was the body. A thumb with no body would have got them nowhere.

A knock, and Zanozin entered, breathless and carrying a folder.

"Menus for the 20th," he announced.

"Any red caviar?"

"Yes, at the Kozak."

"Good lad. How many still to go?"

"Thirty-five, plus eight hotel restaurants."

"Pack it in for now then, and get cracking tomorrow. Results to me by 1.00."

14

"Passport, dollars," said Ivan Lvovich, handing them to Nik, who was now wearing the brand new denim suit he had been presented with.

"Make sure you've got the credit card and tablets. Everything of yours stays here."

Everything, save a photo of Tanya and Volodya safely buttoned into his breast pocket together with two train tickets and a million in the inflated Belarusian currency.

"When you get to Belarus, buy a couple of cases and something to put in them," Ivan Lvovich advised, as they drove to Kiev. "To keep customs happy."

After which they travelled in silence.

Seeing the flyover ahead, Ivan Lvovich told the driver to take the embankment route after Vydubichi, and when they got to the embankment told him to stop while he and Nik stretched their legs.

They walked beside the tranquil flow of the Dnieper. The sun hung low above the hill. Cars sped by. The clatter of a tram was added to the noise of the traffic.

"Nervous?" Ivan Lvovich asked, stopping.

"No."

"Good. Don't smoke, do you?"

"Gave up in Dushanbe."

"Well done!"

While Ivan Lvovich lit a cigarette, Nik surveyed the panorama of island, bridges and multi-storeys.

"You've got Wozniak's number?"

"I have."

"Think you'll remember it all?"

"I think so."

"The fiction is that you, being yourself in the process of defecting, saw him as the very man you needed. You know of money for the taking which one could live very nicely on in the West, and half can be his. How much, I leave to you. Don't overdo it. He's no fool. And make clear that after the share-out, you go your separate ways."

The blue BMW dropped them in the courtyard of a five-storey block, from where they made their way past washing lines and a children's play area to where the Miller Ltd Suspended Ceilings minivan was parked.

The monitors now showed a corridor, a kitchen and a bedroom. In the kitchen Sakhno and a slim girl with fair curly shoulder-length hair were eating a meal. The girl poured wine. Sakhno drained his at a gulp. The girl merely sipped. Putting another bottle on the table, she said something, Sakhno nodded, got to his feet, went into the corridor and disappeared through a door.

"Gone for a leak or a shower," observed Ivan Lvovich.

The girl stood listening for a moment, then slipped into the bedroom. From the wardrobe she fetched a shoebox which she put on the floor and did something to before shoving it under the disordered bed. She then undressed and put on a flimsy negligée.

Sakhno came in wearing only a towel. They kissed. The girl removed the towel, pushed him playfully onto the bed, kissed him, pulled the coverlet over him, and went out, taking the towel with her. Sakhno lay, hands behind his head, staring foolishly at the ceiling.

"The moment of truth," said Ivan Lvovich, passing Nik his mobile. "It's keyed to the number. Bomb under his bed, tell him, and you're waiting below."

As the phone on the bedside table rang, Sakhno looked at it in astonishment, then slowly and reluctantly reached for the receiver.

"Yes?"

"Sergey? There's a bomb under the bed! Meet you outside!"

"Blo-o-dy hell!"

Throwing the receiver aside, he pulled the box out, looked inside, and began to dress.

A film-like sequence followed: Sakhno dragging the girl from the kitchen back to the bedroom, binding her with belts from the wardrobe, dumping her on the bed and shoving back the box before dashing from the flat.

"Second entrance along, Nik. Get a taxi," Ivan Lvovich snapped. "Train's in half an hour."

"This way!" Nik yelled, as Sakhno appeared.

Together they raced to the main road, where Nik flagged down a white Zhiguli.

Only then, heading for the station, did it strike Nik that he and Sakhno were wearing identical denim suits.

15

"Who the hell are you?" Sakhno demanded, when at last they sat breathless in the train.

"I'm Nik. Explanations can wait."

Sakhno gave a feeble grin.

The train moved off.

"Sheets?" inquired the portly conductress who collected their tickets.

"Please."

"Want anything hidden?"

"How do you mean?"

"From customs," she said scornfully.

"No thanks."

"Over to you, then."

Three hours later, Nik was woken by the train grinding to a halt. The lights came on, and there were shouts of "Passport control!"

His, Nik saw with surprise, examining it for the first time, was of the new Russian Federation variety.

"Got yours?" he asked, shaking Sakhno, who, unlike him, had undressed and was using his denim suit as a pillow.

Sakhno rummaged, and throwing a dog-eared Soviet passport onto the table, went back to sleep. Nik opened it. *Family Status –* blank. *Place of birth: Donyetsk, 12 September, 1964,* overstamped in violet *Ukraine.*

A hawk-nosed, green-uniformed blonde checked their photos against their faces, and moved on without a word. She was followed by a tubby, trim-moustached customs man.

"Luggage?"

"Haven't any."

"Stand up."

He pulled out the drawer under Nik's bunk. An ancient newspaper and two cockroaches frozen into immobility by the sudden exposure to light were all it contained.

"Cash? Currency?"

"A little."

"This bloke with you?"

"We're both for Sarny."

"Belarusian roubles?"

"A million."

"Right," he said, and went his way.

By Sarny, Nik was so deeply asleep that the conductress had a job to wake him.

"That's what drinking does," she said. "We're here. You've got five minutes."

He woke Sakhno, and no sooner were they out on the deserted platform than the train moved off.

"What's the time?" Sakhno asked.

"Ten to six."

"Bloody hell!"

They flopped down on the wooden seats in the waiting room.

Sakhno yawned.

"Where now?"

"A night here, then on to Brest and Poland."

Sakhno went back to sleep.

16

Not feeling sleepy, Viktor sat in the kitchen with the light out and a cup of tea at his elbow. He now had the menus of three restaurants – the Kozak, the Mlyn and the Moskva – where Bronitsky could have ordered red caviar pancakes. Zanozin had excelled himself. Tomorrow he would pay them a visit.

17

Nik and Sakhno put up at the small hotel outside the station, slept till four, then toured the few shops Sarny had to offer. The two old-style commission shops were a stark reminder of the Soviet past, and in one of these, with Sakhno looking on in frank disbelief, Nik bought two battered suitcases using their Belarusian toy money.

"What the devil are they for?" Sakhno asked. "But skip that. How about that explanation you promised?"

"When we've got the tickets, we'll go somewhere for a meal."

"Fine," said Sakhno, who was ravenous.

Walking back to the hotel with three hours to go before the train, Nik insisted on buying toothbrushes and toothpaste.

"Why bother with the bloody hotel?" Sakhno demanded, halting abruptly.

"To collect our passports. Look, I'll do that, you wait here."

"Left the key?" the girl asked looking languidly up from her book.

"Yes."

"Hang on. Kla-a-va!"

A sleepy-looking old woman poked her head out of a door.

"Check 35 still has its towels and drinking glasses."

Ten minutes later she slapped down their passports, and with a "Do come again!" returned to her book.

Seeing no sign of Sakhno, Nik broke into a cold sweat. Casting around, he spotted a blue-painted hut with a board saying Bar, and in its gloomy interior found Sakhno addressing a glass.

"What are you having?" he asked.

"Got any money?"

"They take dollars. And they've got port." Sakhno turned to the barman, "One large port, and play this," he said, pulling a cassette from his pocket, and as he made his way back to the table, booming heartbeats filled the bar.

"Bloody tape's blank!" called the barman, replacing it with an old Afghan War number.

Sakhno hauled himself to his feet, eyes flashing fire.

"Take it easy, let's finish our drinks," Nik urged, and to his surprise, Sakhno slumped back onto his seat, clearly drunk or the worse for his recent experience.

"Get him out of here," said the barman, as Nik collected the cassette.

"Got anything to eat?"

"Snickers."

"Give me four."

"You promised to explain," Sakhno grumbled.

"I will when you're more yourself. Just now, we've a train to catch. Bring the cases."

Reluctantly, Sakhno got up, pocketed the cassette, picked up the cases, and made unsteadily for the door.

18

Viktor's round of the restaurants proved unproductive.

The Kozak waiters were reluctant to say anything beyond a "No, don't remember", almost before looking at his photograph of Bronitsky.

At the Mlyn, the manager checked his receipts for May 20th and shook his head. According to a waitress, only two tables had been taken: one by prostitutes celebrating a birthday, the other by men celebrating something else. There'd been no order for caviar pancakes.

The manager and waiters at the Moskva were more welcoming. No one recognized Bronitsky, but that, as someone said, meant nothing, given that there had been a banquet for forty that evening, and people at other tables. Caviar pancakes had indeed been ordered by the banquet party, but in celebration of a wedding anniversary, and that ruled out Bronitsky.

Viktor went early to the funeral, intending to present the widow with white arum lilies, observe the mourners, meet the son, and Ivin, from whom to learn something of Bronitsky, the Defence Consultant – a dismissive "Bronitsky's death has got damn all to do with his place of work!" from Georgiy notwithstanding.

"Meaning what?" he'd demanded, but Georgiy had rung off.

Stuck in a tailback at the turn off for Pechersk, he wondered what the hell was he really supposed to be doing.

Who was he, this Georgiy? Security? That would be logical, but then why all this communication by phone? And why with him, a mere lieutenant concerned with petty street crime? Security had its own special agents. The militia didn't. Too easily bribed. As he might have been, if given special status!

At the next set of lights, he gave up pondering the imponderable, turned his thoughts to the day ahead, and visualizing a fine bronze-handled coffin, switched to the solemn mood appropriate to joining the mourners of one who had departed, or more accurately, flown, this life.

Parking well away from the entrance of the Bronitsky residence, he took from the back seat his tribute of arum lilies.

The door was opened by Widow Bronitsky, all in black, wearing a brooch of black malachite, and weeping as if only just apprised of her husband's demise. The flat was a hive of female activity. An electric mixer could be heard grinding away. Mince was being wrapped in cabbage leaves for the indispensable funeral rissoles.

Exchanging bows with an elderly man – introductions not being the custom at funerals – Viktor settled himself in a corner of the sitting room.

The elderly man, whose shoes bore muddy signs of a journey, sidled over to the armchair next to his.

"Would you be a colleague of Vadim's, if you don't mind my asking?"

"I've had more to do with his widow," Viktor said, conscious of the ambiguity.

"Colleague of Yelena's, then," he said. "I'm his Dad. Ex-miner. Donyetsk region. His Mum couldn't come. She's paralysed. Looks like they're late with the body."

He directed his gaze to the large wall clock framed in polished wood.

"Better see what's happening in the kitchen," he said, getting to his feet.

"Has the son flown back?" Viktor asked.

"Son?" His face took on a haggard look. "It costs a bit to fly from England. No, he hasn't."

The bus with the body arrived at the entrance half an hour late. A splendid coffin of what looked like mahogany was carried from it and placed on two stools.

Viktor stood slightly apart, observing. There were not all that many mourners – perhaps fifty in all – and the cortège was surprisingly modest: two spick-and-span coaches, a black Volga, and a few Zhigulis.

The coffin was returned to its bus, the cortège moved off, and Viktor made for his Mazda, surprised at there being no religious ceremony.

A half-hour crawl brought them to the Baykov Cemetery, where they were joined by a few other mourners bearing flowers and wreaths.

With the grave filled, the mound formed, and the labourers off the scene, there was a passing round of plastic mugs of vodka and meat *pirozhki*. Viktor accepted a glass, which he surreptitiously poured away. As well as Bronitsky senior, two earnest-looking men in expensive suits and several women were in attendance on the widow, who, a little later, made her way from mourner to mourner inviting them to the wake.

Again Viktor followed behind, but now at a faster pace.

Seated at the funeral board, Viktor looked about for the two men who had been standing with the widow, but they were nowhere to be seen.

After a few vodkas, people quietly took themselves off. Bronitsky senior alone seemed set to sit on over his cabbage rissoles, chops, sandwiches and roast chicken. Viktor felt sorry for him. It was as if he, the old Donyetsk miner, had died, not his son.

When no more than a handful were left at table, Viktor asked gently after Ivin.

For a moment Widow Bronitsky seemed at a loss.

"Gone to his hotel. He's got a train to catch."

"Which hotel is that?"

"The Moskva."

Ivin had returned his keys an hour earlier, Viktor was told at reception, but since he'd paid for a second night, he might well be back.

"You have, I take it, a record of everyone who has stayed here."

43

"Of course."

Returning with chocolates from the foyer kiosk, he asked whether a Maksim Ivin had stayed in the second half of May.

The receptionist consulted a ledger.

"Yes," she said at last, "18th to the 21st."

"Single room?"

"Double, but he was alone."

19

Nik expended his surplus of Belarusian currency on the luxury of a sleeper for two. Sakhno, having persuaded Nik to stock up with three of vodka and three of wine, was travelling recumbent. The allowance for travellers crossing into Poland being one bottle of wine, one of spirits per person, or of three bottles per person for two travelling together, Sakhno had made the best choice. And now, having discarded an empty vodka bottle under the table and deposited two passports – his dog-eared one and another of Soviet foreign-travel vintage – on it, he was in his bunk snoring and twisting from side to side. Nik examined the red-covered new-comer. Valid for three more months, it had Czechoslovak, then simply Czech, visas adorning almost every page, the last for ten days in April. At that moment a young border guard entered in quest of passports and tourist vouchers.

Ten minutes later, the coaches were uncoupled and lifted on jacks for the bogies to be removed, rolled away and replaced by bogies of Western gauge.

Nik lay on his bunk trying without much success to calculate just how far Brest was from Dushanbe, then fell to thinking of his wife and son, and the great, slow-moving expanse of the Volga at Saratov. Till now the frontiers between him, Tanya and Volodya had been of the homely, knowable variety, but in less than an hour, it would be different. Belarus, the whole Soviet Union that once was, like everything else, would be behind him. From then on there would be the anticipation of returning. But where to? Saratov? Kiev? In Saratov he had his nearest and dearest; in Kiev the promise of a flat. Once he had a flat, they could come, he'd meet them at the station, take them home in a taxi. But in what sort of a block? How many floors? On which would theirs be? Third would be best. A third-floor flat with a room for Volodya was what he'd ask for. Now the boy had left school, he'd need a room of his own to bring friends and girls back to . . .

The carriage began its noisy descent, connected with the new bogies, then rocked this way and that until finally reunited with them.

Fifteen minutes later the border guard returned their passports. The train slipped from the floodlit glare westwards into the night, and Sakhno slept on.

Waking to his companion's snoring and a Polish dawn, Nik saw that their passports had been dealt with while they slept, and was grateful for the consideration shown.

Fields, villages flashed by to the accompaniment of Sakhno's snores, and the further they travelled, the bigger and better the houses became.

Suddenly, eyes still tight shut, Sakhno reached under the table, setting the empty vodka bottle rolling before locating his carrier of provisions for the journey. From this he took a length of smoked sausage, consumed a considerable portion, skin and all, deposited the remainder on the table beside the passports, and was soon asleep and snoring again.

After returning the sausage to its carrier bag to prevent its falling to the floor, Nik dressed, stowed his bedding away, and sat by the window, entranced by the fleeting scene, and drinking the two cups of tea brought by the conductress.

In Warsaw, where they stopped for twenty minutes, Sakhno woke, shook his head and listened to the loudspeaker announcements.

"What are they saying?"

"It's Polish."

"Fat lot of use you are," Sakhno grinned.

As they travelled on, Sakhno proposed opening a second bottle of vodka, but when Nik demurred, didn't argue.

"Where are we going?" he asked.

"Poznan."

"What the hell is it you want me for?"

"A job. Do it, collect your share, and that's it."

"And that's why you got me out from under back there?"

"Exactly."

"Right," was the surprisingly limp response, followed, with a grin, by "I daresay I'll survive, if others don't".

Nik seemed suddenly to see it all. He was interpreter-factotum, Sakhno was hitman. They were an operational team. Their abstract objective having been set by Ivan Lvovich, they would now receive concrete instructions from Wozniak in Poznan.

Phoned from the station, Wozniak said he would pick them up. They were to wait by the taxi rank. They then sat sunning themselves for a good half hour before he turned up, in an ancient Mercedes, and whisked them off to a little café on the outskirts, where they were quickly served with beer and plates of salad. Stocky, moon-faced, he inquired politely about Kiev, and Sakhno spoke animatedly of new shops and restaurants while Nik kept prudently silent. A pork and cabbage dish came, and more beer.

"Going to give Polish vodka a try?" Wozniak asked Sakhno, who perked up visibly.

"And would you mind savouring it over there, while Nik and I talk business."

"No problem," said Sakhno getting to his feet, and moving to the corner table, to which Wozniak brought vodka and pickled cucumber from the bar.

"Stick these away till later," Wozniak said returning to Nik and slipping him two blue passports.

"They're in the names of Niko Tsensky and Ivo Sakhnich, citizens of the new Yugoslavia, with visas for Germany. There's DM three thousand each in these envelopes. In an hour from now you take the electric train to Germany. Speak German?"

"I studied it."

"In Berlin – the tickets are in the passports – you change for Koblenz. In Koblenz you stay at the Hotel Mauer. It's cheap, good and no distance from the station. There you sit back and wait to be contacted."

"Who by?"

"Don't worry, he'll be one of us. And how are you getting on, you two?" he asked, inclining his head to where Sakhno sat staring at an empty glass.

Nik said nothing.

Wozniak smiled

"Good luck, anyway! Though God knows what with. My part's played. We'd better be off."

Wearily, reluctantly, Sakhno rose and joined them.

20

Viktor's plans for the funeral had come to nothing, and but for the discovery of Ivin's earlier stay in Kiev, the day would have been a complete loss. At least his direct or indirect involvement in Bronitsky's death now seemed as good as proved.

Viktor walked for an hour or so before returning to the Moskva, where he had left his car. He looked into the foyer. The receptionist was now a middle-aged brunette with hair lacquered into a balloon-like eminence.

"Where can I get a coffee?"

"The fourth-floor buffet, if it's good coffee you want."

The coffee came with a tiny bar of chocolate. He ordered a second cup, and while waiting, moved to a window seat. There was the Coca-Cola balloon, and there, opposite the Central Post Office, the State Vehicle Inspection booth.

As he left, he glanced at the menu. Apart from sweets, beverages and drinks, one could have chops, chips, chicken and, to his amazement, *red caviar pancakes*!

Instead of going to his car, he made his way over to the little enclosure formed by red road barriers, and found that the balloon cable was attached to one of three large gas cylinders. There was no-one keeping an eye on them.

Carrying on down to the fountains, he crossed to the SVI booth on the other side of the square, to see how conspicuous the balloon was from there. It was, very. He'd done well, he decided. Now to Moscow, to tackle Ivin.

"Go for two days," said Georgiy, when Viktor phoned him that evening.

"The tickets will reach you at District tomorrow morning. But if you sense Ivin is involved, arrange to meet again, and come straight back."

While waiting for his tickets, Viktor sent for Zanozin, instructing him to check who, on the night of the 20th-21st, was on SVI duty, Independence Square, then interview him.

He then phoned Ratko and invited him to coffee.

"Very grand all of a sudden! Got sugar?"

"Yes, Major."

"On my way."

Viktor kicked his overnight bag under the table. He had yet to break it to Ratko that he was off to Moscow that evening.

21

Nik was surprised how much German he remembered. At Berlin Zoo he not only managed to inquire the time of the train to Koblenz, but understood the reply.

"Well?" asked Sakhno, standing with their cases.

"Platform 2, Track 3, in half an hour."

A station cleaner in baggy overalls walked past pushing a little yellow cart. Like the man at the information desk, he was wearing a name tag.

Watching him, Nik had the curiously detached feeling of a diver lowered into a different world, amongst fish of a fabulous order. All too soon, in a month or so at best, those above would pull on his life line and haul him up. Meanwhile, anything could happen.

Sakhno grinned.

"Well done. Not your first foray into foreign parts, then?"

"No, I've been to Africa," said Nik, returning to the surface. "We'd better get going."

The train was spotlessly clean, the seats like sofas. At half-hourly intervals a trolley came round with tea, coffee and snacks.

"Though addicted to drink, I still have eyes to see," Sakhno said, turning to Nik with a smile as the trolley passed. "You got two envelopes from your Polish pal as well as passports. Could they be envelopes of money, and one of them for me?"

"Yes, and you shall have it at Koblenz," promised Nik, thinking uneasily what Sakhno would spend his Deutschmarks on.

In their room at the Hotel Mauer Sakhno tossed his case onto the bed better placed for the wall-mounted television, and headed for the shower.

Five minutes later he appeared, wet-haired, carrying two glasses.

"Wine or vodka?"

"Wine."

"To our safe arrival," he proposed. "Now where's my envelope?"

He counted the notes carefully.

"It'll do for a start. And more to come, no doubt."

He knocked back a second glass, and got into his denim suit, slipping the envelope into a bulging breast pocket.

"You may as well leave your passports," Nik suggested. "They won't get pinched."

"Sod that! What's mine goes with me! – I'm going for a stroll. See if I can't find some sausage for supper. You do as you like."

"Hang on, we're expecting a visit."

"You are, not me. You're duty dog," he quipped as he went out, banging the door behind him.

Exhausted and feeling a complete idiot, Nik finished his wine, lay down on Sakhno's bed, and watching some pop singer, fell asleep.

22

After a night disturbed first by Ukrainian then by Russian customs Viktor arrived in the sweltering heat of Moscow in a somewhat jaundiced state. He'd travelled in company with a businessman intent on proving, despite small response, that life was on the upgrade, who, after two bottles of beer, passed out as if they'd been vodka, and stayed out from Kaluga on, until roused by the raucous loudspeakers of Moscow.

Dressing, Viktor was horrified to see his automatic and holster all too obvious in the unzipped bag under the table. Customs had twice got him out of his berth to look under it, without noticing the unzipped bag.

He checked in at the Kiev Hotel, where four hundred thousand roubles per night for a single room made a big hole in the apparent fortune of eight hundred thousand roubles received as travelling expenses. "Staying how long?"

"One night to begin with."

"Extensions must be made before eleven the next day, otherwise it's vacate and settle."

"Not settle in advance?"

She smiled.

"We have your passport. The militia registration fee of one hundred and twenty thousand is extra."

Deciding to start with the lesser fry on the chance of getting a line on Ivin, he rang Bronitsky's two other colleagues, and receiving no reply from either, rang Ivin.

"Yes?" a pleasant female voice answered.

"Could I speak to Maksim Petrovich?"

"He's out at the moment. But leave your number and he'll call you back."

"When do you expect him?"

"In about half an hour."

"Might I come over and wait?"

"Know where to come?"

Before setting out he hid his automatic and holster at the bottom of his bag and shoved it under his bed.

In the thrill of the chase he forgot his bad night, but the Stalinesque blocks of Kutuzov Prospekt, arrayed like a scowling bevy of hefty colonels, provided a depressing setback. A reek of melting asphalt and vehicle exhaust contributed to the impression of entrapment, but as he searched for the right block, his confidence returned.

"Where are you off to?" demanded an elderly caretaker, ex-army, if the combat suit was anything to go by, seated behind a glass partition in the hall.

"Ivin, Flat 62. I'm expected."

The caretaker indicated the lift.

It was clean, quiet and provided with a mirror.

One day there'd be a lift where *he* lived, though it would soon be squalid. This one had air freshening.

The faint sound resulting from pressing the bell suggested double doors of unusual solidity. He waited a minute, then rang again, and once more.

He returned to the hall intending to ask the caretaker if he'd seen Ivin, but the caretaker had gone, leaving his book open on the table.

He'd left his mobile in Kiev, not expecting it to work in Moscow, and it took some time to find a phone. When he did, it required tokens, and it took another fifteen minutes to find a newspaper kiosk that sold them.

"No one is available to take your call," said an answering machine when at last he rang Ivin's number. "Leave your name and number, and we'll call you back."

He rang the other two Kievites again, but still no answer.

Returning to the hotel, he rested until seven, then rang all three numbers, but to no avail.

At the buffet on the second floor he paid fifteen thousand roubles for a salami sandwich and salad.

Waking at around 3 a.m., he had another go at telephoning, but might just as well not have.

Next morning, he packed his bag, announced he was leaving and put down five hundred and twenty thousand roubles.

The receptionist consulted her register, then gave him his passport and four hundred thousand roubles' change.

"Your bill's been paid," she said. "There's just the one hundred and twenty thousand registration fee."

"How do you mean?"

"Paid. End of story."

"Who by?"

"No idea. I've only just come on. You can pay again, if you like . . ."

A mistake. It must be. He didn't know anyone in Moscow. And yet someone must be the poorer for that amount.

Leaving his bag in a station locker, he bought another ten tokens and wandered the city telephoning until the last of them was swallowed by Ivin's answerphone.

At 20.00 he went back to the station, bought the Moscow papers, retrieved his bag, had a coffee, and made for his platform.

The blonde conductress finished wiping the boarding handrail before taking his ticket.

"Viktor Slutsky?" inquired a tall, fair-haired man pleasantly, looking into the compartment where Viktor was sitting next to a grimey window, too weary to change into his track suit.

"Yes?"

"Going already? And without getting your interview? Come, I've a car outside."

"But this is the train my ticket's for."

"Here's another for tomorrow. Single sleeper. Bring your bag. It's an hour's drive, then supper . . ."

The Volga was of a type he'd never seen, black, with darkened windows. Tall Fair Hair sat in front with the driver. He sat alone in the back.

23

When Nik woke at 10.00, the television was showing a film. There was no sign of Sakhno.

Feeling hungry, he went down to the hotel restaurant.

"The chef goes off at 10.00," explained a smartly-dressed elderly man sitting alone over a mug of beer. "But I can heat you something in the microwave."

The simplicity and the homely warmth of the place were disarming. He opted for Frankfurter and chips and a mug of beer, and had scarcely sat down at a table when the man brought his order, wished him *guten Appetit*, and went back to his own beer.

Nik found himself thinking of Tanya and Volodya, made unhappy by his telegram. Still, there was nothing he could do, and they would have to grin and bear it just as he had. As in the Soviet past, bright new futures were elusive. Which didn't mean that they wouldn't come, only that some cost was involved. And in these infant days of Slav capitalism, anything good – bright future included – was extremely pricey. Free, gratis and for nothing was a concept of the past.

At getting on for midnight and after another beer, Nik went to his room, looked out of the window, wondering, not for the first time though now somewhat more relaxedly, where the hell his companion had got to.

24

Viktor sat with Tall Fair Hair, Refat, as he now knew him, and Yura, their tubby driver, at a richly spread table on the summer veranda of a fine dacha.

"Wine or vodka?" Yura asked, assuming the role of cupbearer.

"Wine, please."

"Juice for me," Refat confirmed, adding, for Viktor's benefit, "I'm sorry to say."

Yura served tomato salad, sausage and cured fillet of sturgeon.

"Dig in," said Refat. "There's a hot course to follow. We can sup to the song of the nightingales, and at dawn's first rays, we can sleep."

The mystery of the hotel bill now seemed solved, but it left Viktor the unhappy feeling of having been bought. And for what?

"Cheer up!" said Yura. "You could now be in your filthy carriage having a torch shone in your face and being asked for your passport. So let's drink! To friendship!"

Refat clinked his glass with the others.

"It was Ivin you came to talk to, wasn't it?" Refat asked suddenly.

"Yes."

"Show him the photos, Yura."

They were of three men lying face upwards on a blood-soaked carpet, one of them the man seen by Viktor with Widow Bronitsky at the cemetery.

"Is that him?" Viktor asked.

"Surprised you didn't recognize him."

"A good moment to drink to his memory," said Yura, pouring vodka for himself and wine for Viktor. "Death catches up eventually, however hard you run."

"What questions did you have for him?" Refat asked.

"How did you know it was him I'd come to see?"

"He rang from Kiev saying he'd been photographed at the cemetery and was afraid they were out to kill him. I assume it is Bronitsky's death that you're investigating?"

"Yes," said Viktor, "but I didn't see any photographs being taken, and I was there at the cemetery."

"He'd intended to stay on a few days after the funeral. Instead he flew straight back home, where his wife found him, when she returned from visiting a friend."

"Who was it answered when I phoned?"

"One of us."

Refat sipped his apple juice.

"Look," he went on, "you, understandably, are cagey. But we're both of us Russians. This splitting into different countries is politics. We, you and I, are working on the same case. We, too, want to know what happened to Bronitsky. It wasn't, as you may think, wicked Moscow that did him in after the Staff HQ trouble. Not one of us here had the slightest interest in seeing him dead. I can support that with facts, only you'd have to keep them to yourself. Though the Russo-Ukrainian treaty concerning inter-Security-Service co-operation provides sufficient justification for our present meeting.

"You can take these photos with you for your report, and you can put down the extra day to Major Krylov – that's Yura here – of the

Moscow Criminal Investigation Department. An exchange of questions and answers is all I'm after."

"Fine," said Viktor, overcome with curiosity.

"So why the sudden interest in Ivin?"

"Three days ago I discovered he'd been staying at the Moskva on the key dates. I have reason to believe that he and Bronitsky ate at the buffet there the evening Bronitsky died."

"Spot on," said Refat. "Good work. But why complicate things for yourself?"

"How do you mean?"

"By having an office at District."

"Why not? It's mine."

Refat forced a smile.

"To go back to Bronitsky. Was it you who prevented the body's being flown to Voronezh?"

Refat seemed both to know too much and yet to put wrong questions. Viktor poured himself wine and drank.

"You have, you say, proof of Moscow's non-involvement."

"We'll leave it," said Refat, as Yura entered bearing a pan, from which, with a flourish, he served them each with three cylindrical pancakes.

"Mustn't let them get cold."

Cutting into his pancake, Viktor found that it was filled with red caviar.

"Yes," said Refat, "it was us, Ivin, Bronitsky and me, eating together in the fourth-floor buffet on May 20th.

"For your ears only, Bronitsky in his Staff HQ days was a good friend to us, and as Presidential Adviser even more so. He'd have prevented that second delivery of Ukrainian tanks to Pakistan, but for the fact that the ship had sailed . . .

"The flat above Ivin's was to be Bronitsky's new home in a couple of weeks, and we were discussing his future. He left about midnight – I having phoned for a taxi – intending to look in on a colleague in Bastion Street.

"We traced this colleague, but too late. Accidental death. Geyser gas leak exploded by lighted match was the official verdict. In fact, he was killed by a home-made bomb.

"I believe he was the organizer of all this, if not the actual killer. The balloon part would have called for extra help, and may not have been his handiwork at all. Who knows? Anyway, he's dead and buried. One more funeral, and we can close the file."

"Whose?"

"The bomber's . . . It's the classic variant: cut the first two links and there's no causal chain."

"And the balloon?"

"If we ever got who did that they'd probably be small-time, acting, they'd say, on the instructions of the chap who got blown up. But let's eat."

Viktor helped himself to more pancakes. Clearly Refat took him for Security – the remark about his having an office with the militia was proof of that – and the extent to which he was confiding in him was flattering. The explosion in Bastion Street, which was on Viktor's patch, was news indeed.

"Keen shot?" Refat asked.

"Yes."

"Come and see our range."

They followed a lighted path to a tunnel-like underground range a short distance from the house.

Refat produced long-barrelled small-bore pistols, and they fired at targets lit for two seconds only. Refat scored well. Viktor, who had not stuck to apple juice, less well.

"Back to the table, or off to bed?" Refat demanded.

"Back to the table."

"Now for your questions," said Refat, as Viktor was helping himself to tomato salad.

"Why were you bringing the body to Russia?"

"We weren't. It wasn't us. The logic of it escapes me completely.

Unless the idea was to implicate Moscow. What sort of plane was it?"

"An AN-26 of Belarusian Airlines."

"And the cargo?"

"I don't know. Crates, cartons."

"And weren't interested?"

"It was the body I was interested in. You can find out from Voronezh what the cargo was."

Refat grinned.

"According to Voronezh customs, combine harvester spares for Sunrise Agricultural Suppliers, who paid the duty and collected. Only there's no such firm. Did what you saw look like harvester spares?"

"No."

"If you get anything further on that flight, do please let us in on it. You'll find us grateful. We're as keen as you are to get to the bottom of this business."

When Viktor woke it was midday, and brilliantly sunny.

Downstairs he found Refat sitting reading the paper. They drank coffee together, then went up to Viktor's room.

"You'd better have this," Refat said, producing Viktor's automatic and holster from the bedside cupboard. "We took charge of it at the hotel before the chambermaids went through your bag." Bending to the drawer, Refat brought out a second Tula Tokarev. "And accept this one as a souvenir and mark of friendship."

Viktor looked puzzled.

"Why do I need two?"

"It's what's called a 'backfirer'."

Extracting the magazine, he showed that the rounds were inserted nose to rear.

"What's the point?"

"It was an old favourite with Stalin. Your would-be killer becomes a suicide case. We did a weapon-switch on some thugs recently, and are now four the fewer. It's vital, of course, not to get them mixed. See, the modification's stamped with three 9s instead of one.

"Now take it easy, put your feet up, see if you can think of any more questions, and when it's time to eat, we'll shout. Oh, and if you'd like to pop down for the papers. I've finished with them."

RUSSIA AND UKRAINE – NEITHER PEACE NOR WAR? ran the eye-catching *Izvestiya* headline. It was a question, it appeared, of determining the frontier, or, more exactly, of the two sides being able to agree where it ran.

25

Woken by shouting in the street below, Nik rushed to the open window in time to catch "*Pidory nemyetskiye!*" – "Rotten German sods!" – delivered in a familiar voice, and saw Sakhno standing at the hotel entrance haranguing two men – one of them his obliging waiter of the evening before, now clearly the manager – and, dominating the entrance, a long, black limousine.

By the time Nik got to the front entrance, Sakhno and the vehicle had disappeared.

As Nik stood looking this way and that, hoping to God Sakhno hadn't been arrested, he suddenly came around the corner of the hotel, puffy-faced, red-eyed, carrying a well-filled plastic bag in one hand, and a Walkman in the other.

"What's up?" he asked, seeing Nik was barefooted.

"Your shouting. You woke me!"

"Let's get to the room. I've had an arseful of these bloody Germans! Up on their hind legs, not a word of Russian between them! You'd think they'd won the war!"

"Wouldn't they let you in?"

"They will now," Sakhno said, throwing back the thick glass door.

The elderly manager watched with a frown.

"Why all the fuss?" Nik asked, when they reached their room.

"They were the fuss! Didn't like the car."

"What car?"

"The limo I bought yesterday. They had some beef about its blocking the entrance. Instead of being grateful for having it parked there. It's a damned sight smarter than this hole."

"Is this the car that was there when you were effing and blinding?"

"Yes, not one of their titchy VWs, and now at the back blocking the car park exit. So they can laugh that one off!"

He put the Walkman on the window-ledge and the carrier bag on the floor beside his bed.

"Where did you get the money?"

"The envelope. Four thousand DM was what they wanted for the car – I got it for two thousand eight hundred."

"Where did you spend the night?"

"In the car. Lost my way. This morning I found the station and came on from there."

Whatever next? Nik wondered. A plane hijack? With Sakhno out of funds anything was possible.

"Can you lend me two hundred?"

"Reading my thoughts?"

"Should have made it five hundred, perhaps."

Nik handed over four fifties from his wallet, cheered by the thought that Sakhno seemed equal to anything.

"I'll show you the town. It's not a bad place. We'll follow our noses, you having first treated me to breakfast."

"Treat yourself. Breakfast's downstairs and included in the room price."

Alone in the dining room, they stretched self-service to include preparing their sandwiches for the day.

"Some country this," Sakhno conceded, tucking in. "Pity they don't learn Russian at school."

The car, all five metres of it, looked fine from a distance, but on closer inspection showed signs of extensive body work and efficient re-spraying. A surprising feature was that it had seats only for the driver and a passenger, and a rear door opening onto a vast load space level with the top of the two seats.

"Well?"

"Fine, except for passenger space. You could put in extra seating."

"Sort of thing the Germans are good at. Just a question of money. Hop in."

"Stop at the entrance. I'll tell the old boy we'll be back by 2.00, in case anyone wants us."

Nik stepped from the car with a curious sense of pride. He was a different person, with a different past, a limousine and personal chauffeur. In the foyer he was brought speedily back to earth.

"You park that hearse outside my hotel again, and you and your chum are out on your ear!" the elderly manager announced grimly.

26

On his way home from the station, Viktor left a note for Ratko saying he would be in at lunchtime.

It was misty, and after the heat of Moscow, mild with a light breeze.

His night in a single sleeper had left him fresh and ready for work, border guards and customs having let him sleep, seeing the militia warrant card left ready with his passport. His bag with the two automatics had been under his bunk.

Ira, all smiles and kisses, prompted the suspicion that something was up.

In the living room Yana was asleep in her cot. On the table, expensive flowers, a bottle of Crimean muscat, and a telegram.

Some relative must have turned up, or be on their way, and would have to be met. Resigned, he reached for the telegram, and to his amazement read: HAPPY BIRTHDAY DARLING = DELAYED EXTRA DAY = HOME TOMORROW MORNING = LOVE VIKTOR.

Ira flung her arms around him.

"Thank you," she whispered. "Yesterday would have been better, but all's ready for tonight. Have a good trip?"

He nodded.

"You've got a letter. In the kitchen."

No stamp, no address, only his name.

"How did it come?"

"Left in our post box."

The envelope contained a small slip of paper, and under yesterday's date and a telephone number, "No offence, I trust. All the best, Refat."

Pocketing the slip of paper, he felt as if he'd been scanned by some vast X-ray machine. It left him with a nasty metallic taste in his mouth and a vague, almost childish sense of resentment.

"Shall I make some coffee?" Ira asked.

"Please. I must get back to work."

"But you'll be home by 7.00?"

He nodded.

At District, he found Zanozin waiting patiently.

"Major Ratko said you'd be back by lunch," he said, getting up.

"How's it going?"

"On duty on the night of the 20th-21st was a Sergeant Voronko, who's now out of town, earthing up potatoes for his mother, but will be back on Independence Square tomorrow night. Anything else I can do?"

"Yes, ring round all Bastion Street officers, find out who had a flat fire on his patch in the second half of May. Get the details."

When Zanozin had gone, Viktor stuck his tiny immersion heater in a glass of water, and gazed out at the trees.

Away from Refat's green-eyed gaze and calm assurance, he felt the need to check the accuracy of what he'd been told, and his instructions to Zanozin were a start in that direction. After which he had another simple task for him to get to work on and report back on by 6.00.

It was irritating enough to have forgotten his wife's birthday, without having some stranger remembering for him and acting accordingly. There was a touch of taunt and warning about it. As if to say, we've got your measure. Crimean muscat was just right, but roses weren't. Ira preferred chrysanthemums, but perhaps there weren't any.

Slipping the photographs of the murdered Ivin into the Bronitsky file, he took paper to write a full account of all that had happened in Moscow, including what Refat had told him. But after staring for some five minutes at the blank sheet before him, he thrust it aside. Some things were better committed to memory.

In the drawer where he had left it, his mobile rang.

"Welcome back. How was it?"

"Not quite as expected."

"How so?"

"Ivin's been murdered. The other two weren't at home."

"Interesting. Anything else?"

"The SVI man on duty on Independence Square that night has been traced, and I'm interviewing him tomorrow."

"Who's dealing with the Ivin murder?"

"Moscow CID. They've given me their crime scene photographs."

"Got onto them, did you? There was no need . . ."

"They got on to me, before I knew."

"Well, Federal Russian militia assistance is something always worth having. You're sure it was CID, not Security?"

"Pretty sure."

"Right. Ring when you've seen the SVI chap."

Viktor drank his coffee, then looked in on the cadets. Zanozin was seated at a desk, writing hard.

"Any joy?"

"May 23rd, Block 15, Bastion Street, Flat 23, incident at about midnight. Gas explosion. Flat gutted. Owner lost his life."

"The owner being?"

"Veresayev, Nikolay Petrovich, Colonel, Border Troops HQ, sole registered occupier."

"Did our man attend?"

"No. The fire brigade was summoned by neighbours, and we were only notified when the fire was out and the body found. Our man sealed the flat next morning, but didn't go in, the body having been removed."

"Good lad!" said Viktor, waxing genial. "Just one more job. Pop round to the Moskva, note who spent the night of the 19th there, and report back."

Zanozin darted off, and Viktor looked in on Ratko.

"Ah, there you are! Your Zanozin keeps pestering: 'Seen the Chief, Major? Seen the Chief?' I'm Chief here, I tell him, but it's water off a duck's back. What's he like for you?"

"First rate."

"Like a decent drink?"

"Not on duty and driving."

"I, too, am on duty, but all right, you drive, I'll drink. It's five years to the day my wife died. Not exactly in mourning, nor exactly happy, that's me."

So saying, he tossed back his plastic beaker of Smirnoff, returned beaker and bottle to his safe, and flopped down on his swivel chair.

For an hour they talked of this and that across Ratko's littered desk, until there came a knock at the door.

"Yes!" bawled Ratko.

"Seen the Chief, Major?" asked Zanozin, half in, half out.

"Hell's bells! This here is Lieutenant Slutsky. Me, I'm the Chief! How many more times?" laughed Ratko.

"Sorry, Major."

Returning to his own office, Viktor looked through Zanozin's two pages of hurried scrawl, and spotted *Sibirov, Refat Abdulkarimovich, Room 316*. The assiduous Zanozin had even noted his passport details.

"You deserve a medal!" he said. "Off you go. See you tomorrow." Having chauffered his mildly tight major home, Viktor set off for home himself. It was 7.15, and remembering it was Ira's birthday supper, he put his foot down.

27

Sakhno was not in the least abashed at discovering he'd bought a hearse.

"Wouldn't be seen dead in one, but now I'm not bothered," was his comment.

Its thirst for petrol was of the order of a Slav's for vodka. Sakhno thought the fuel pump must be at fault, and one evening decided to check. But finding nothing wrong, he gave up. After all, Nik was paying for the petrol, as well as for everything else.

In the days that followed they explored Koblenz and its surrounds, and Deutsches Eck, at the confluence of the Rhine and the Mosel, became a favourite spot for lunching off their breakfast sandwiches.

Twice, late at night, and to Nik's surprise and envy, Sakhno drove off into town. Lack of German notwithstanding, Sakhno seemed the more at home and at ease here. Of growing concern, beyond worry on the score of Tanya and Volodya, was the failure of anyone to make contact.

One morning, after breakfast, he asked the elderly manager how much they owed.

The elderly manager tapped away at a keyboard.

"Nine hundred and sixty DM," he said.

Which, deducted from their remaining seventeen hundred and fifty DM, left Nik aghast, until he remembered his American Express card.

Sakhno, carrying sandwiches wrapped in paper napkins, joined him in the foyer.

"All set?" he asked.

"Where to today?"

"Somewhere in town, then into the country."

The somewhere proved to be a dingy suburb some distance from the city centre, where, pulling up outside a church and saying he wouldn't be a minute, Sakhno disappeared down a dustbin-cluttered alley, only to return, clearly displeased, and drive on, swearing.

"What's up?" Nik asked, but received no reply.

They were driving along a narrow forest road when Sakhno braked abruptly and performed a three-point turn, causing a fine new Mercedes to screech to a halt. Nik expected signs of annoyance from the elderly driver, but instead they received an affable nod. Maybe he thought they'd missed their way to a funeral.

By the time they returned to the hotel, Sakhno was a little calmer. Seeing him take two bottles of wine from his carrier bag, Nik fetched glasses from the bathroom – why did the chambermaid persist in putting them back there? – but Sakhno gestured that they were not needed.

Reaching again into his carrier bag, he brought out a round loaf of rye bread, which he placed on the glass tray reserved for the water carafe.

"Got a knife? Well, get one from the old man – you're his blue-eyed boy."

Sakhno took the knife Nik brought and used it to cut out a small circle of crust. Into the resultant hole he poured the contents of the first bottle, then, more slowly and with exaggerated care – as if filling a mine with explosive – the contents of the second. He then replaced the circle of crust and passed Nik the knife.

"You carve. Blow yourself up, and I take all!"

"Cut it like a cake?"

"Yes."

They ate the whole loaf in silence, Sakhno wearing a look of serene satisfaction. The wine seemed more than usually potent.

"Where will you lie low when the job's finished?" he asked suddenly.

"How do you mean?"

"To stay alive. The doers of jobs tend to get disposed of. It's safer that way for the men behind them."

"Where will you?"

"Not saying, even to you."

Getting up and slipping a cassette into the Walkman, he flopped back on to his bed.

It was the heartbeats tape.

"You played that at Sarny. What is it?"

"Knowing when and where to get me out from under, you'll know that too. So don't play the innocent, Nik," Sakhno answered, falling asleep and snoring.

After a while the cassette ran out.

28

Sergeant Voronko resumed duty three days later than expected, having caught cold and recovered, predictably, with the earthing-up of the potatoes, tolerance on the part of SVI being every bit as firmly rooted as the venerable oak at the door of Mother Voronko's hut.

On the morning of June 9th, when at last Viktor interviewed him, it cost Voronko an effort to think back to the night of the 20th-21st May, and when he did, he swore. That was when he'd been summoned to some other post – he couldn't remember which – only to be stood down when practically there. And to cap it, while he was away, some bastard had stink-bombed his booth. So he'd smoked a cigarette, then taken himself off to the Borisopol Highway access post, and played beggar-my-neighbour for the rest of his shift. The balloon had been there when he left the post, but he'd had other things to think about when he got back.

Back at District, Viktor set Zanozin to discover which SVI post had summoned Voronko to attend on the night of the 20th-21st, who was on duty then at the Borisopol Highway access, whether Voronko had, in fact, joined them at cards, and finally, who had decontaminated the SVI booth, when and using what.

Zanozin jotted it all down, smelling strongly of fish.

"Celebrating last night?" Viktor asked.

"Drinking beer till 4.00."

"You've got till lunch tomorrow. Sort that lot out, and the beer's on me."

Zanozin moved faster than expected, and well before lunch came bursting in on Viktor and Ratko drinking tea in the former's office.

Viktor gave him a chair and tea.

"Well?"

"No one radioed Voronko. I've checked everyone then on duty. He was, though, at the Borispol post from 3.00 to 6.00, but not playing cards."

"Oh no, of course not," laughed Ratko, "just studying the latest copy of *Duty calls* over a cuppa."

"Like us," said Viktor.

"Only we're not SVI."

"Epidemiological Control," continued Zanozin, "reports decontaminating dibetamethyl at the third attempt. Dibetamethyl is used in military anti-gas training. They smash a capsule at your feet and it's on with your mask in fractions of a second."

"Permission to fall out, Comrade Major?" Viktor asked, tongue in cheek, getting to his feet.

"Fall where you like so long as you drop the 'Comrade Major' – it's even worse than 'Ratty'!" said Ratko, slapping Viktor on the shoulder and taking himself off.

"Let's go for a beer," Viktor suggested, when he and Zanozin were sitting in the Mazda, "And decide what next."

"This flat waiting list, Comrade Lieutenant," Zanozin ventured. "I'm thinking of getting married."

"Over to the Major on that one."

"I've tried."

"Keep at it. He'll move in the end, if only to get shot of you!"

That evening Viktor rang and reported the latest to Georgiy.

"You've got more out of SVI than I'd have thought possible."

"But not who took Voronko from his post."

"Maybe nobody. Maybe he went to see some woman, came back, dropped the stink bomb, and nipped off for a game of cards. One sure check would be the SVI band monitor."

"Where do they hang out?"

"Near Arsenal metro station. Access is tricky, but I'll do what I can for you."

29

Next morning found Sakhno off colour, disinclined for breakfast and unable to face what Nik took up to him.

"Sorry about yesterday," he said, squinting up at Nik, "and hitting the bottle. I'll lie here a bit longer, then I'll be fit."

The cassette, Nik saw, going over to the window, was no longer in the Walkman. So Sakhno must have left his bed to remove it. The air, through the open window, was cool and fresh. It was drizzling.

"I deserve a good punching," Sakhno said.

"That business with the loaf . . ."

"Antipersonnel mine, you mean. Inserting the charge was a monthly ritual with us in the army. Until there was no one left to do it with . . ."

"How do you mean?"

"Once, when on mine-clearing, we'd all got stoned. Next morning, seeing me fit for damn all, as now, they left me to sleep on. Trouble was they missed a tension wire, and up they went. You couldn't get me some coffee?"

He drank it slowly, then showered for a good half hour before returning, looking not much better.

"Come for a drive."

"You should be taking it easy. Anyway it's raining."

"I've got to. We won't be long. You drive."

It was Sunday, and Koblenz seemed deserted.

Ordering which turnings to take, Sakhno brought them to the familiar dingy suburb and the equally familiar stopping place outside the church and opposite the narrow dustbin-cluttered alley.

"Wait here, and lend me a hundred."

Reluctantly Nik took the money from his wallet.

"I'll pay you back," said Sakhno, and staggered off up the alley.

Nik watched with increasing unease, and five minutes later set off in pursuit, abandoning the hearse as hardly worth stealing.

Sakhno, he saw from afar, was standing gesticulating to one of a small group who was gesticulating back, apparently in deaf-and-dumb language. Rain torrented down, and when next he looked, Sakhno was hurrying back.

"Where," Nik asked, "did you learn deaf-and-dumb language?"

"From my parents. Mother interpreted for deaf-and-dumb delegations abroad. Four languages, four systems."

70

"And you?"

"Just three. And here it's next left!"

"What were you doing there?"

"Buying cigarettes."

From then on they travelled in silence, except when Sakhno, Koblenzer now to his fingertips, announced which turning to take.

30

"Rise, shower and breakfast!" instructed Georgiy. "Call you in twenty minutes."

Viktor heaved himself out of bed and made his way to the bathroom, clutching his mobile. From the bedroom a wimpering. As soon as Yana was off night feeds, he could return to their good broad bed. The sofa was leaving its mark on his back. But better that than a wakeful night.

Refreshed by a cold shower, he was drinking coffee when Georgiy rang.

"How are we?"

"Better."

"Lesi Ukrainki Boulevard, round tower, know it? Good. Military entrance at 9.00, warrant card at the ready – they've got your name. Room 32's what you ask for, after which keep your card out of sight. Go through to the courtyard, and turn left. The second iron door has a keypad lock. The magic number's 3516. You then go up to the first floor, where you tell them that you've had your car stolen, and that your Dad, General Borsyuk, has arranged for you to hear a playback of the SVI channel for the night in question, on the off-chance of its proving helpful . . ."

A junior lieutenant, who looked too intelligent to be a soldier, led him to a vast tape library.

"What's it you're after?"

"SVI for the night of the 20th-21st."

He brought a large reel, put it on the console, searched, found the place, and passed the headphones to Viktor.

The recording was chiefly of background hiss interrupted every now and then by a message.

Twelve! Blue Mercedes, jumped lights, heading your way! Get him!

Two! Time check please.

0030 hours. Spoken to Stepan?

Yep. Friday we go fishing.

General alert! Red Samara, Registration: KIA 89-71, stolen Pushkin Street.

Then, after a long interval:

Seven! Proceed at once to 11!

Received and understood.

Viktor listened intently.

Three! Red Samara just gone through – could be the one.

Sod it then!

A long silence, broken by:

Seven! Attendance no longer required. Return to post.

Viktor got the lieutenant to make him a copy.

31

Nik went down for a frankfurter and a mug of beer. When he returned, Sakhno was lying on his bed staring at the ceiling, and the air was heavy with a familiar smell that he couldn't immediately place.

"Like some sausage?"

Eyes wide with amazement, Sakhno tried to turn his head, but was not able to, and suddenly it all came back – cannabis, that was what the room reeked of, like a Tadzhik bazaar! And Sakhno was the worse affected for having taken it on top of wine. Nik opened the window wide. It was damp and chilly, but no longer raining.

Drugs, drink – God, what a combination! What the hell had Ivan Lvovich been thinking of? Tablets against his perhaps becoming a menace were beginning to make sense.

In need of a drink, Nik went down for another beer.

Next morning, there was a knock on the door, and a thin, hawk-nosed, middle-aged man looked in. He wore his sandy hair parted in the middle, and the jacket of his grey, much-laundered, vaguely rustic suit was in the nature of a tunic. Seeing Sakhno asleep, he suggested that they went down for a coffee.

"I'm Heinz," he said. "A name seen on tins. Wilhelm Heinz."

His Russian was faultless. He'd arrived from Kazakhstan some ten years back with his Russian wife, who, having learnt German, left him for a local pharmacist. A human story, briefly told, inspiring trust and sympathy.

Joining a dozen or so others at breakfast, they sat at a window table with a view of rain.

"No objection, I take it, to my eating for your friend," Heinz smiled. "I imagine you've settled in."

"I think so."

"And your friend?"

"No problem."

Heinz made himself a ham sandwich, and stirred sugar into his coffee.

"Tomorrow you move on. Which means a collecting in of passports – your friend's Yugoslav and Ukrainian, and your own?"

"I've got mine here," Nik patted the bulging breast pocket of his denim jacket.

"So nip up and get his."

Abandoning his coffee, Nik went and shook Sakhno awake, only to be gestured to a jacket yielding no more than a Ukrainian foreign travel passport and a small packet of cannabis.

"Your Yugoslav passport, where's that?"

Sakhno opened one eye.

"Lost it."

"Where?"

"Deaf-and-dumb place."

"Mislaid while drunk, more like," was Heinz' comment. "Does he drink a lot?"

"A fair bit."

"Well, let him."

Breakfast finished, he handed Nik two new green German passports.

"These make you ethnic Kazakhstan Germans, like me," he said with a laugh. "And here," passing him a card, "is your new address, paid up two months in advance."

"Only Sakhno speaks no German."

"Like many ethnic Kazakhstan Germans. Which is why Germans and Turks don't like them."

"Why the Turks?"

"The Turks work hard, learn German, but don't get passports so easily. So, congratulations on becoming German."

Taking his empty plate, he helped himself to more ham and sausage, cheese and rolls, evidently enjoying his meal on the house.

"Anything from Ivan Lvovich?" Nik asked

"Don't know him," said Heinz, clearly surprised. "My instructions were to give you the passports, and that's what I've done, and needn't have, now the Soviet Union's a thing of the past."

"So passports, and that's it."

"Passports and a flat."

"And then?"

"No idea. Wait and see."

Returning to their room, Nik examined the new passports in the names of Niklas Zenn and Theo Sachsen.

The latter being still asleep and snoring, Nik let him lie.

It was 10.30, so if they were leaving today, he must settle the bill before eleven.

Shutting the door quietly behind him, he made for the stairs.

32

Told of the tape, Georgiy said he must hear it, and Viktor was to hold everything until he had, making a copy on Ratko's twin-deck recorder – to be delivered by Zanozin, as later directed.

At 2.00, when the copy was ready, Victor confirmed as much to his invisible Chief.

"Tell Zanozin to be at the Lenin monument, Bessarabian Market, at 3.00," he responded. "Someone will inquire the way to Repin Street and the Russian Museum, and he's to accompany that someone up the avenue to Repin Street, handing over the tape as they go."

A someone who might well be Georgiy!

Allowing Zanozin a five-minute start, he jumped into his Mazda, and ten minutes later, was walking towards the Bessarabian Market, having left his car outside Cinema House.

And there, at 2.55, was Zanozin standing at the monument, gazing this way and that, like an indifferent spy or a restless lover.

Darting into the underpass, Viktor surfaced at the bread shop midway between the Lenin monument and Repin Street, and stationed himself just inside.

Ten minutes later, he saw Zanozin heading up the avenue in company with a close-cropped, auburn-haired young lady, half a head shorter than he, in sun glasses and blue dress. Zanozin passed her the tape, which she slipped into her bag, then returned wearing the foolish grin of the smitten male.

Viktor's mobile rang.

"So we're at Cinema House."

"No, just passing."

"Hopefully in the course of duty. Call you in an hour."

Georgiy's tone, when he rang, was congratulatory.

"Good stuff! Which we must squeeze dry. See if your SVI sergeant recognises the voice. And that red Samara might well be connected with the folk we're after. Theft of a vehicle in the furtherance of crime smacks of tradition, but you never know."

Voronko, Zanozin reported, was due on duty in an hour and a half's time, at 1800 hours. Viktor set him to find out what had become of the red Samara stolen on the night of the 20th-21st, placed four chairs side by side under the window, and lay across them. This was how he had snatched sleep in the army, but now he wanted to stare at the ceiling and think, and the hard chairs were good for his back.

Shortly before 6.00 Viktor set off for Independence Square, taking the cassette and a portable tape recorder borrowed from a colleague.

"Still on about that night?" Voronko asked wearily. "Like I said, I got called out, then played cards."

"Yes," Viktor reassured him, "and now we've got supporting evidence."

They went into the booth, where it was quieter, and Viktor played the tape.

"That's Stepan!" Voronko said cheerfully.

"Stepan who?"

"Grishchenko, Senior Lieutenant . . . Like I said."

"What you said was that you didn't remember."

Voronko shrugged.

Asked about the red Samara, he found his memory equally deficient. With sometimes a dozen vehicle thefts a night, you couldn't remember them all.

Viktor got him to radio control for Grishchenko's whereabouts.

"Off duty till tomorrow night," said Tinny Voice.

Returning to District, Viktor told Zanozin to get Grishchenko's address.

"That car," said Zanozin. "I forgot to tell you."

"Well?"

"Found at 0800 hours on the 21st in Bastion Street, outside the block with the gas explosion."

Bastion Street again! In some amazing way, Refat in distant Moscow saw more than he did on the spot!

"Want the gen on this Grishchenko?" Zanozin asked.

"Yes, and quick about it."

Viktor sat back, his mood a strange mixture of weariness and triumph, then his mobile rang. It was Georgiy.

"Well?"

"It's Senior Lieutenant Grishchenko on the tape. I should be seeing him in an hour or so."

"Good lad. How about the car?"

"It looks as if it was 'stolen in furtherance'. It was found next morning in Bastion Street outside – " He stopped, remembering that he'd so far not mentioned the supposed gas explosion and its victim.

"Outside where in Bastion Street?"

"A flat that blew up killing the owner. Shortly after Bronitsky died."

"Tell me more."

"Gas explosion is the official version, but an explosive device is the more likely explanation. The victim was a colonel at Border Troops HQ."

"When did you find all this out?" Georgiy asked, clearly surprised.

"Only just now."

"In the course of that duty stroll near Cinema House?"

"Yes," said Viktor, not expecting to be believed.

"Well, good for you!" was the unexpected response. "Quite a linkage of events. And the address?"

Viktor gave it.

"So things are moving and again in the Pechersk direction," said Georgiy, with a note of satisfaction. "Ring you later."

Pocketing his mobile, Viktor felt only fatigue. Any sense of triumph was gone. Georgiy was no fool. He'd be beginning to have doubts. But things *were* moving and gaining momentum. It was time he investigated the late colonel's friends and colleagues, as he'd been told not to in the case of the late general. Still, a colonel was different from a general.

A knock. It was Zanozin.

"Grishchenko lives in Podol. I've rung, he's not there, and his wife doesn't know when to expect him."

"Right," said Viktor. "At 8.00 tomorrow, phone round, run him to earth, and we'll get questioning."

33

The one-room flat, found for them in Euskirchen, was, though not spacious, comfortable, the L-shape affording scope for a degree of privacy.

"Could be partitioned into three," said Sakhno, "but why no curtains?"

Nik shrugged.

The five-hour car journey from Koblenz, with the engine baulking at every steep climb and many departures from the route drawn for Nik by the hotel manager, had left them exhausted.

"I," said Sakhno, "am bloody hungry and there's damn all in the fridge."

"What did you expect? Wine? Hors d'oeuvre?"

"Hors d'oeuvre, yes. Wine we could have bought. Any Deutschmarks left?"

A telephone rang.

Looking, Nik found the instrument on the floor.

"Settled?" asked a voice.

"Just arrived."

"Take it easy. Job tomorrow. Ring you at 8.00."

"What – " Nik began, but the caller rang off.

"Someone for us?"

"Work starts tomorrow."

Opening the window, Sakhno rolled a joint from his supply of cannabis, and lit up.

Nik took himself off for a breath of air. It was raining lightly. Coming to a general store, he bought sausage, bread and milk for their supper.

34

Setting off for work, leaving wife and daughter still asleep, Viktor lighted on the bag he had taken to Moscow, and thinking of the curious weapon it contained, tossed it out of harm's way with the case of unwanted wedding presents atop the corridor cupboard.

He drove slowly, past fellow block-dwellers heading for the metro. Braking sharply before the main road, he sensed a shifting in the boot, but knowing it to be empty and swerving clear of a plank with projecting nails on the road, he drove on. When he again braked sharply, this time at Southern Bridge, the impression was stronger of something having shifted. Maybe the spare wheel had come adrift, and once clear of the bridge and roundabout, he decided to check. Opening the boot, he froze with horror. Doubled-up in it was the corpse of a man in canvas overalls. No shoes. Brown socks.

Banging the boot shut, he switched on his warning lights and tried to think.

An ancient Mercedes drew up alongside, and a bald head appeared.

"Can give you a tow," it offered. "Twenty dollars. Got a rope."

"Thank you, no."

"I've got a corpse in my boot," he informed Georgiy.

"Well, there's a nice good morning! Since when?"

"Some time in the night. Cropped hair, canvas overalls. Military-looking. No shoes."

"Splendid!"

"What's splendid about it?"

"Shows you're getting warm. Now's the time to be careful."

"What do I do with the body?"

"Let me think."

"And cart him round Kiev while you do?"

"Not for long. He'll still be fresh. Behave as normal. I'll ring you."

Viktor parked and went up to his office.

An hour later, though it seemed an age, Zanozin came and reported.

Grishchenko was not at his home address, having, as likely as not, spent the night at his dacha. Should he ask his wife for the address and go out there?

Viktor agreed, but then, realizing that if Georgiy rang, he mustn't involve Zanozin in disposing of the body, thought better of it.

"We'll wait till he's back, but keep phoning. Anyway, tonight he's on duty."

Two hours later Georgiy rang.

"Not, I trust, distracting you from work. So what you do is, take the Zhitomir road, and at the Korchaginets bus stop – the twenty-two-kilometre post, roughly – it's sharp right onto a dirt track skirting forest. You'll see patches of oil, then a house. The garage will be unlocked. Dump him in there."

"Won't someone be about?"

"Not till evening. Just the odd passer-by. So off you go, and ring when you're clear."

35

Shortly before eight the phone rang.

"Niklas Zenn?" asked a man's voice.

"Yes."

"Listen. By 12.00 be at Monschau. Lunch at Masha's in Flusstrasse, proprietor one Pogodinsky, Aleksandr Ivanovich. Treat him like someone who owes you. Establish who he's transferred, or paid interest to, on profits for the past ten years. Play it by ear, your friend drinking and playing up as he likes. Ring you this evening."

"How do we get to Monschau?"

"You buy a road atlas," said the man, and rang off.

"Time to get up?" asked Sakhno.

"Not just yet."

Nik took a shower, then slipped out to buy both road atlas and coffee.

"Where today?" Sakhno asked.

"Lunch in a restaurant."

"Then?"

"Back here. I'll explain as we go."

Monschau was a fairy-tale town of brightly-painted gingerbread houses on a tiny river. Shops, restaurants were all cosily miniature. A sign pointed to the Mustard Museum.

"We could leave the car here," Nik suggested, seeing a car park.

"No, right outside, let's make the man's day."

The hearse blocked the whole frontage.

"Think it matters, my not wearing a tie?" Sakhno asked, smiling maliciously.

A bell rang as they opened the door. The restaurant was empty.

"More like a snack bar," Sakhno muttered.

A grey-haired man in dark trousers and white chef's jacket greeted them in German.

"A Russian restaurant and yet they speak German," Sakhno grumbled.

"No problem," came the ready response in Russian, "I've not forgotten it."

"What about the menu?" Sakhno persisted.

"I'll translate. Do sit down."

"You must be Herr Pogodinsky," said Nik.

Pogodinsky tensed.

"You know me?"

"Only from friends. They spoke well of your restaurant."

"We don't often get Russians here," he said, adjusting the place settings. "I can do you a good pork chop with onions . . . Or there's calves' liver . . . Fresh vegetables . . ."

"Fine," said Nik. "Two chops, two salads, carafe of vodka."

"Pickled cucumber?"

"Need you ask?" Sakhno snapped.

Pickled cucumbers and carafe were quickly on the table, and Pogodinsky went to prepare their order.

"All a bit Soviet periodish," said Sakhno looking after him. "Though then he'd have had a whole host of cooks and waiters . . ."

"It's not terribly busy."

"Probably a money laundry."

Sakhno filled their glasses.

"Let's hope we strike it rich!"

Glass and slice of cucumber half way to his mouth, he paused for Nik to respond.

The bell rang, and an agitated German appeared in the doorway and proceeded to harangue them.

"What's he on about?" Sakhno asked.

"Can't get by the hearse."

"Bloody man!"

Sakhno got up, brushed past the German, and the hearse moved out of sight. A coach full of old age pensioners glided past the window, and until the hearse returned, there was a pleasant view across the river to little houses hung with ornate name signs.

"Why make their buses so bloody wide!" demanded Sakhno, returning wrathfully to the table, and downing vodka.

Nik was beginning to have qualms about having to provoke this inoffensive little old man, proud proprietor, chef, waiter all in one. Only this was not the world he'd known as a soldier, but a more complex one where so much, so many people – this simple, genial, little old man included – were not what they seemed. So why worry? Do as they were told, and all would become clear.

The chops, which were enormous, were served with mushroom sauce, a mountain of chips, boiled beetroot and a ball of green spiced yellow rice.

"More vodka?"

Pogodinsky's eyes, as Nik met them, were blue, strong, alive, smiling, thirty years younger than their owner.

"A carafe."

"We wouldn't be owing money, would we?" Sakhno asked Pogodinsky as he brought the carafe.

He looked from one to the other aghast.

"Who to?"

"Niklas Zenn, say," said Sakhno.

Pogodinsky nodded, gazed forlornly about him, and retreated to the kitchen.

"Kills me, your politeness," said Sakhno.

"Drink up, don't worry," Nik advised soothingly. "We can't all go chucking our weight about."

"Good health, then!" said Sakhno, downing his vodka and crunching cucumber.

The ensuing silence, calming at first, began to weigh on Nik. Casting around for loudspeakers or tape recorder, and seeing neither, he was about to go in search of Pogodinsky when the latter brought him an envelope.

"Anything else?" the old man asked with a look of great weariness.

"Two coffees and the bill."

"Well, what's the score?" demanded Sakhno.

The envelope contained a cheque for ninety thousand DM in favour of Niklas Zenn, which, as Pogodinsky brought the coffee, Nik put out of sight.

"And the bill?"

"You're not serious?"

"We are!"

Pogodinsky made the bill out, and Nik paid over the forty-seven DM it amounted to.

Pogodinsky stood holding the money as if at a loss what to do with it.

"May I suggest you don't try cashing it in Monschau," he said suddenly. "Go somewhere bigger. Düren or Aachen."

Though not clear why they should, Nik nodded.

Sakhno finished what remained of the vodka, and they left.

The hearse moved slowly away, restoring to view the well-loved beauty and tranquillity for so long part of Pogodinsky's unpretentious but far from simple life.

Pulling off the road, Sakhno leant his head against the door and closed his eyes. Nik got out and strolled amongst the pines until himself overcome with weariness. Climbing into the back of the hearse, he stretched out in the coffin space.

The surrounding pines made early evening seem like night.

36

Viktor spent most of the next day in his office awaiting events and telephone calls. At least twice, and secretly laughing at himself for so doing, he went and checked the boot of his car. There were no new corpses. Nor did Georgiy phone.

Zanozin looked in several times to report that Grishchenko had neither appeared for duty nor returned home. When, towards evening, Georgiy rang to say that the body in the boot was that of Senior Lieutenant Grishchenko, the news came as no surprise.

"And tomorrow morning why not just pop back to where you dumped him? Look the house over. You never know what you might find."

"How about who lives there?"

"Lying in the morgue. They opened fire instead of the door. Go early. You won't be challenged."

Setting off next morning, after once again checking the boot, he was surprised how few people there were about, until he remembered it was Saturday, when normal folk would still be abed. He remembered, too, that he'd not told Ira he was going, but no matter, he would be straight back.

The garage door was half open, as also the wicket beside the main gate of the house. He came first on an empty kennel, then a dead Alsatian, still attached to a running-leash cable.

The solid oak door yielded at a push, and he entered. The silence was unnerving. Where, then, were Georgiy's watchers? The short hall terminated in another open door. He glanced in, then mounted the creaking wooden stairs.

The attic had been converted into a lounge with three settees, a large dining table and wide-screen Sony television and, in the far corner, a desk littered with invoices, letters and copies of the glossy weekly Itogi.

The desk drawer, which he opened with his handkerchief, contained a notebook, a Dictaphone, a couple of cassettes, and a stainless steel box with handles, such as syringes for Granny's injections had been kept and sterilised in, when he was a boy. This one, he saw, lifting the lid, contained a scalpel, three tiny, different-toothed saws, and surgical forceps.

He returned the handkerchief to his pocket – others had been here disturbing prints before him. He would take what seemed of interest.

His phone rang.

"How's it going?"

"It's odd. No security, but any amount of stuff."

"So?"

"Thought I'd take the best of it back to the office."

"Four plus out of ten! Four for back to the office, but you get a plus for effort."

"Office not the right place?"

"No, home, and ring when you get there. Security's present, but you're not seeing it."

A tiny video camera in a corner of the ceiling! Kilometres away someone was watching, or recording, as with SVI radio traffic!

Sensing suddenly that it was time to leave, he swept everything off the desk into a large carton, throwing in the surgical box and contents of the drawers for good measure, and carried it out to his car.

Taking another look round on the ground floor, he discovered an iron manhole in the kitchen leading to the cellar, but was unable to raise it.

He pulled the wicket gate to behind him, shut the garage doors more securely, and left.

Some five minutes after the red Mazda had returned to the smooth asphalt of the Zhitomir highway, the Miller Ltd minivan drew up outside the house. The driver opened the garage doors and reversed in.

37

Returning to Euskirchen, thoroughly chilled by their night in the hearse, Nik and Sakhno went straight to bed.

Nik woke at noon. The sun was shining, German birds were singing. He made coffee, made sure that the cheque was still safe in the pocket of his jacket, discarded on the floor, then roused Sakhno.

Sakhno was all for cashing the cheque in Cologne, but Nik insisted on Düren as closer and offering fewer temptations.

Düren was a drab little town. They left the car in a two-storey car park, and soon found a bank.

"Slip me ten marks, and I'll wait in that café," said Sakhno, "while in you march, singing your head off, as they say in the army."

Nik handed the cashier the cheque and watched her fingers dart over her computer keyboard. Suddenly they stopped.

"It's dated the year after next," she said, passing it back over the counter.

"Give me two hundred," said Sakhno, sitting before a tall glass of beer.

"Haven't got it."

Nik showed him the cheque.

"Bloody man! We'll have his guts for garters!"

Finding Masha's shut, they found their way to the back. Sakhno hammered hard on the solid door, then forced the catch and entered. Nik, who had been keeping watch by the dustbins, followed.

Sakhno, when he caught up with him, was in the kitchen eating ham from an open fridge.

"Can't have gone for long, leaving all this food. Look upstairs."

Nik made his way up to a carpeted landing with a watercolour of St Basil's on the wall. Of three doors, the first opened into a small bedroom: wooden double bed, dressing table, small television, two faded still lifes, metal-framed photograph of a middle-aged woman. Next, a tiny study: desk, two walls of bookshelves, revolving easy chair, single window giving onto the embankment. Then to the sitting room, where he found Pogodinsky, hanging by a strap from a hook which had supported the chandelier, now on the floor beside an overturned chair.

"Come and eat," said Sakhno, sitting over beer and ham at a corner table in the restaurant, "we can do ourselves well till Pogodinsky comes back."

"Pogodinsky's still here. Upstairs. Hanged."

"Sod the bloody fool! Well, dig in all the same!"

Nik ate, contemplating the black, fire-guarded void of the hearth and doing his best not to think.

Bringing beer and a glass, Sakhno poured for them both.

"Any cash about?"

"Haven't looked."

"I'll have a go. Finish the beer first."

Sakhno rummaged noisily upstairs, and eventually came down with a bulging carrier bag and a tortoise.

"Found it under his desk . . . Can't leave it to starve . . . Seventy marks, that's all the money . . . No sign of a safe . . . There's a chequebook so the bank's where the cash is. But let's go. We've sat here long enough."

It was getting dark as they made their way back to the hearse, Sakhno cradling in his arms the carrier bag which now contained the tortoise.

They left Monschau at about 10.00, and drove for a long while before realizing that they were lost.

"Game for a second bivouac in the forest?" Sakhno asked, and as Nik said nothing, passed him a flat stainless steel flask from the carrier bag.

Whatever it contained was pleasantly bitter to the tongue, aromatic and very strong – like Riga Balsam.

"To hell with the wretched man!" Sakhno said, reaching for the flask. "But at least we shan't freeze!"

38

The kitchen was becoming increasingly like a night office, but Viktor's sleepless hours there were not especially fruitful. No sooner did the Bronitsky case seem on the point of getting somewhere, than it raised fresh questions and puzzles. And Georgiy the Invisible, while clearly more in the picture than Viktor, appeared in no hurry to share what he knew.

The notebook he'd brought from the house outside Kiev contained as many Moscow telephone numbers as Kiev ones. Its owner – of whom Viktor knew no more than that he was dead – had lived in both capitals and dealt with, amongst others, Ivin and Kozitsky of the Bronitsky circle.

He rang Georgiy.

"Since you ask," Georgiy said, not, apparently, surprised to be rung at such an hour, "the notebook will have belonged to Vasily Prorokov, also known as 'Mr Blessed', and now reposing in the morgue. A real crook's crook. Came to these parts from Tula a year ago. With him on the slab are the District Tax Police Chief, Voronezh, his younger brother, and A.N. Other, carrying no papers and so far unidentified. I'll ring you on that one."

Viktor entered Crook's Crook Prorokov on his diagram of Bronitsky connections, then lit the gas to boil a kettle.

Ira appeared in the half-open door, barefoot and in her nightdress.

"Shouldn't you get some sleep?" she whispered.

"Just going to."

39

Nik stood at the window with a glass of beer, gazing gloomily down at the empty, rainy, Euskirchen street, thinking of Tanya and Volodya.

"Let me have twenty," said Sakhno.

Nik pulled two notes from his shirt pocket and passed them over.

"It's boring here. I'm going for a drive."

"Fine."

The door banged, and a little later there was a hoot as the hearse turned the corner.

Nik was about to boil water for coffee when the phone rang.

"How did you make out with Pogodinsky?"

"He's hanged himself."

"So you overdid it."

"No, all went smoothly."

"Were you seen when you found him hanged?"

"No."

"Leave any evidence of your visit?"

"No."

"Right. Stay put. Ring you shortly. No need to mention my call to your friend, when he gets back," the voice added, leaving Nik to conclude that they were being observed.

When the man next rang it was to ask if they had brought back any papers.

"Sakhno did," said Nik.

"Have you seen what?"

"No."

An accusing sigh greeted this admission.

"Go now and see! You've got twenty minutes. Whatever it is – notebooks, chequebooks, credit cards – have it ready by the phone."

The carrier bag was by the radiator, so, too, a saucer of water and the tortoise.

The carrier bag yielded two tins of black caviar, Produce of Astrakhan; a generous portion of salami; a bottle of Smirnoff and one of Absolut. The rest was indeed personal stuff: two notebooks, a chequebook, letters, a fat pocketbook and two sets of colour photographs. The notebooks were in German and Russian, the photographs of people whose faces meant nothing to him.

Sakhno's professionalism in making this collection came as something of a surprise. Nothing had been said about seizing documents, and it hadn't occurred to Nik to do so.

"Well, what have we got?" asked the telephone voice.

Nik reported.

"Got a pen? Write down these names: Slonimsky, Kurz, Weinberg. Any mention of them, make a note. I'll call back."

The next twenty minutes Nik spent searching the diaries, and when the man rang, was able to give phone numbers for Kurz and Weinberg.

"Got the tablets still? Good," the man said, and rang off.

40

Viktor set off for an afternoon walk, giving his red Mazda a glance and the guard a friendly nod as he went, and made his way to the Shelkovichnaya Street *gastronom* where he and Zanozin had been for a beer. Zanozin was now on temporary loan to Ratko, assisting in a case involving arms sales.

Viktor took his large coffee over to a stand-at table in the window and was watching the people pass in the sunlit street, when Georgiy rang.

"What's new?"

"You tell me."

"I'm going to. Listen. The day after tomorrow you fly to London for a conference on money-laundering. I'm having a passport delivered to you at the office by 6.00 this evening."

"I don't speak English."

"There'll be an interpreter."

"But what's the point?"

"It's a three-day conference. You have a six-day visa. So the point is to have a full and frank talk with Bronitsky junior. I'll ring and brief you further. This is work, not a jolly, so get yourself into the mood."

He was past being surprised by anything. Go to London, he was told, so to London he'd go. He was beginning to tire of the whole thing. And not least of being given a case, and from the word go denied a mass of detail known to others who were in on the case as well.

He'd have to bring back something for Ira and Yana. How surprisingly practical he was all of a sudden!

Returning to his office, Viktor found Zanozin seated at his desk.

"Got a surprise," he said smiling and patting a large brown envelope.

It contained a photograph showing a badly burned corpse in a room destroyed by fire. "Veresayev, Nikolay Petrovich, Colonel, Border Troops HQ," Zanozin explained.

"Who took it?" Viktor asked, examining it closely.

"Find me a flat, and I'll tell you," laughed Zanozin.

"Tell me, and I'll find you a couple."

"It was taken by On the Spot TV. They're well in with the fire brigade – they've got a direct line. One of the On the Spot crew had his own camera."

"How did you find out?"

"Spoke to the firemen."

"Brilliant! Carry on like like this, keep your nose clean, and you'll have your flat!" Viktor grinned. "But I'm not sure where this photograph gets us."

"Look at his hands."

Viktor took the print over to the window. The body lay arched, right arm flung back, left arm reaching forward. The tips of all fingers had been burnt away, but while the left thumb was more or less intact, the whole of the right thumb was missing!

"Have you seen the TV footage?"

"Hasn't been kept. This photo's all there is."

"Well, thanks."

When Zanozin had gone, Viktor looked at his watch. 3.55. Pending the arrival of his passport, he would give his mind to thumbs.

41

As it grew dark, and Sakhno had still not returned, Nik marvelled at his managing to make twenty marks last so long.

He looked around for the tortoise and was relieved to see it still motionless before its empty bowl. Then the phone rang.

"Why try to fool me?" asked the man.

"How do you mean?"

"You've left a hell of a lot of evidence at Masha's . . . You're going to have to ditch your pal. Then we'll help. We can't get both of you out of this. Slip him two of the tablets, and when you've done that, ring 48-04, and I'll tell you what next."

The dialling tone followed, and for a while Nik stood, still foolishly holding the receiver to his ear.

The tortoise had withdrawn its head into its shell. He hoped it wasn't dead.

What evidence had they left? The man was talking gibberish! Ditch Sakhno, indeed!

He opened the window. The night air was amazingly warm. Hearing a vehicle, he leant out, hoping to see the hearse, but was disappointed. The drizzle was like a tepid shower.

The phone rang, but he let it, and went and made coffee.

After a while the phone rang again, and this time Nik answered. If the flat was being watched, they would know he was there.

"How are we?"

Nik said nothing.

"Sorry if you're put out. No need for any tablets. Just pulling your leg. You left nothing too incriminating."

Nik swore.

"That's the way – let off steam! And now you need paper and pen . . . Tomorrow's route and the new target address.

"The house," he continued, after Nik had read it all back, "has got cameras and security and is not to be approached. What you're to do is buy en route four kilos or so of frozen fish. This you chuck over the wall when you get there, then come straight back."

"A four-hour drive just for that?"

"And one that you'll be doing more than once – so think long-distance! But here's your pal coming back. Good luck!"

Sakhno was in a cheerful mood. He put down lettuce for the tortoise, which the tortoise showed no interest in, keeping its head retracted, and offered Nik a smoke, which he refused. Told what was proposed for the next day, he showed no surprise and simply nodded.

42

The plane took off from Borispol for London at the early hour of 7.30 a.m. Viktor left his packing to Ira, and arranged for Zanozin to spend the night at their flat, then drive the car back to District from the airport.

Sitting in the kitchen, Viktor checked the three hundred dollars travelling expenses in one pocket, and in another Ratko's fifty dollars for a pair of red braces, any change from which, Ratko had said, he was to keep.

"You must buy some new socks – yours are mostly holes," came Ira's voice. "And where's the bag you took to Moscow?"

"Top of the corridor cupboard."

Minutes later Ira came in, handed him the curious automatic and asked, "Is this the bag you're taking?"

Weighing the gun in his hand, he looked around for somewhere to put it. The dusty space between kitchen cabinet and ceiling looked promising, and wrapping it in a tea-cloth, he put it there.

Georgiy rang.

"All set?"

"Almost."

"Mind on the job?"

"Practically."

"You'll have three hours on the plane to collect your thoughts. Good luck! Ring when you get back."

Zanozin turned up shortly before midnight, produced a bottle of Odessa cognac from his briefcase, and sat in the kitchen, where Viktor joined him, having checked his bag and looked in on Ira and Yana.

"Ever been to London, Comrade Lieutenant?" Zanozin asked.

"Moscow, Chernovtsy, Zhitomir are the only places I've been. And for God's sake call me Viktor."

"You could bring back some beer."

"What sort?"

"Any good sort."

Time flew to the point where Viktor judged it wise to switch from cognac to mineral water. At 6.00 they went down to the car. The route to the airport was happily straightforward.

At Gatwick he emerged from immigration control to see a young lady displaying a card with his name wrongly spelt, and speaking no Russian. He followed her out to a black Ford Mondeo which they drove to London and the Kensington Park Hotel. Here she saw him to his room, presented him with a plastic folder of conference literature, and left.

Viktor sat on the bed regretting that he'd not brought a dictionary, when the bedside phone rang.

"Welcome to London!" said a pleasant female Russian voice. "I'm Vika, from the Embassy, your conference interpreter. I'll come over and explain the literature if that's all right."

"Please do."

He felt suddenly happier, and taking in the mini-bar and wall-mounted television with remote control, even more so.

43

It was after midday when they started for Trier and it took almost five hours to get there, after time spent locating a fish shop, and arguing what to buy and how much to spend. Sakhno was all for small sardines at seven DM a kilo. Nik, in default of specific instructions, preferred proper fish to what Sakhno dismissed as "gobies in tomato sauce". In the end, they bought four kilos of outlandishly named and astonished-looking fish. As they continued on their way, they were slowed by rain.

From Trier they took the Luxembourg road, and in five or so kilometres spotted the narrow tarmac track they had been told to look out for. Parking the hearse amongst trees, they set off on foot along the track with the fish. The rain had eased, but the air was humid and heavy.

A quarter of an hour brought them to tall gates in a tall brick wall, where, hearing a car approaching behind them, they darted into the woods.

A crimson Jaguar pulled up, the gates swung slowly back, revealing the two-storey villa with red-tiled roof, satellite dish and naval-style squashed-sphere aerial that lay beyond.

The gates swung shut, and as if taking that as a signal, the rain returned.

One by one Nik threw the fish over the wall near the entrance, where, he argued, they would be more conspicuous.

"Mission completed," Sakhno laughed, and they trudged back through the rain to the hearse. Then added, "We do, I suppose, get reimbursed for outgoings on fish."

"It's their money we've been spending."

"Which leaves food-and-drink expenses incurred delivering fish."

44

The conference venue was the Hilton, a half-hour walk from Viktor's hotel.

The first session, "Suspect Totals in Inter-Bank Transfers", conducted by a young lady from the Bank of England, left him cold, in spite of Vika's conscientious interpreting. During the break for watery coffee other delegates glanced at his name tag and passed on. "Finding it interesting?" Vika asked archly as they stood together apart from the rest.

"Yes, but beyond me," he confessed.

"So let's get you in with some of the more worth knowing," she said, Young Communist organizer to her fingertips, marching him over to two thickset men standing smoking in the window: one a Swedish Home Office official concerned with drug proceeds, the other an Economic Crime specialist from Germany. Vika spoke at length with both in English, but did not translate.

"I hope you don't mind," she said later. "I said I was your secretary and invited them to dinner at the Plaza at 7.30 this evening. Don't worry, it's on the Embassy. Our Commercial Councillor will do the talking. We need the contacts."

"We?"

"Your embassy. You're a patriot, aren't you?"

He didn't answer.

"No need to sit the whole meal out. When you're bored, just get up and go."

The second session was as unfathomable as the first, but a welcome, if unexpected diversion was provided by the late arrival of Refat. Viktor looked around for him at the end of the session, but he was no longer to be seen.

"Pick you up at 7.00," said Vika. "Think you can find your own way back to the hotel?"

Black taxis, red buses, a vast and varied mass of people. He had the feeling of acting in a foreign film. Any minute the action would start. There'd be a shoot-out, a car chase. It was absorbing, alien, until suddenly the homely M of a McDonald's caught his eye.

It would be good, he thought, munching a Big Mac, to meet up with Refat, if only over a drink of tea or coffee. He respected the man, found him genuinely interesting, without quite knowing why. He was serious, truthful, straightforward. He had a proper sense of his own dignity and integrity, where Viktor was beginning to wonder if he himself any longer did. He had the impression of being played with, turned into a puppet. Even his own embassy was using him as cover.

At reception he was given his key and an envelope. "Good to see you. Have news. Refat, Room 602", said the note it contained.

"Not locked," Refat called in response to his cautious knock.

Wearing a smart, well-tailored navy-blue suit, he shook hands warmly, ushering Viktor into a room the mirror image of Viktor's own.

"Weren't expecting to see me here, were you? But I thought I might see you. I'm glad we've met up. Have some juice."

He fetched a carton of apple juice from the fridge. There were glasses on the table.

"Since when this interest in money-laundering?"

"Since yesterday."

"So a couple more days won't hurt, and might even be good for your general education. Do you speak Polish?"

"No."

"Pity, but don't worry. Hang on a minute."

Going to the phone, he dialled a number.

"Wojciech, come and join us . . . You'll like Wojciech," he said, returning to his chair. "He's the decent sort of Pole. Likes a drink. Hasn't got my liver."

There was a tap at the door.

"Not locked."

It was a short, slim man of about forty who entered, wearing jeans and a light jacket over a black T-shirt.

"Got the photos?" Refat asked, introductions completed.

Taking an envelope from an inside pocket, Wojciech passed Viktor some photos. None of the faces was familiar, and one in a photo of three men at a café table had been blotted out.

"Our man in Poland," explained Refat. "Ukrainian Security requested assistance for 'two visitors from Ukraine', including the provision of passports. Most interesting, though, was that these two were shadowed to the German frontier by two other Ukrainians who kept phoning back to Kiev."

Wojciech now took up the story.

"They were armed – hence our interest – and the expectation was that they were going to knock the other two off before the German frontier. Instead they turned back. So far we've a score of five CIS corpses, all carrying forged passports. One we identified before burial, the rest we buried all the same. But supplying graves gets tedious!"

"I like your turn of phrase," said Viktor.

Wojciech laughed.

" 'Live with the wolves, howl with the wolves,' as you Russians say!"

"Enough said," laughed Refat. "But to be serious. We have, as they say, reason to suppose a connection between these two and the Bronitsky balloon flight. We're trying to locate them, but Germany's a big country. If they've gone to earth, that's probably it. But if they're looking for something or somebody, they'll pop up sooner or later."

"What could they be after?" Viktor asked.

"Ask that of whoever sent them. These two maybe," Refat said, pointing to a photo of a hefty fifty-year-old with cropped blond hair and a slightly younger, stocky man with toothbrush moustache. "Anyway, see what you make of them."

"Oughtn't we to go out somewhere?" Viktor suggested.

"You and Wojciech, yes, but better not in company with me," said Refat.

Agreeing to meet the next day at 5.00, in Refat's room, Viktor and Wojciech set out in quest of "real Irish ale".

45

After the trip to Trier, Nik woke at 3.00 in the afternoon, and finding Sakhno still snoring helped himself to yoghurt from the fridge and put the kettle on. It was then he noticed, just inside the door, a brown leather case which had not been there earlier. On the point of releasing the old-fashioned catches, he suddenly thought better of it.

"That case by the door – is it yours?" he demanded, rousing Sakhno to some semblance of wakefulness.

Springing out of bed, Sakhno came and squatted down beside it.

"Could be a bomb. 'No more fish, thank you very much! Love, Trier.' Stand well back in case it is."

With a resounding click Sakhno released the first catch, then the second, then gently laid the case on the floor.

"Bloody ages since I handled a bomb, and it's still a bore."

Gingerly he lifted the lid.

"Well?"

Grinning broadly, Sakhno produced the barrel and butt of a rifle, a night sight and a silencer.

"No money. So they're buggering us about! But here's a box. Ammunition! So what's this lot for, Nik?"

"I'm sure the man will phone and tell us."

"He'd better, the bastard!" snarled Sakhno, dumping the parts back in the case. "And it's time you got dressed and went shopping! I have been driving all night! Food, drink and lettuce for my tortoise is what we need. Cos lettuce, if they've got it."

The phone rang.

"Consignment to hand?" asked the man. "Right, tonight it's the same place, after dark. Friend Sakhno shins up a suitable tree and picks off the dogs. On your way back, ring 546-33 from Trier, and tell the answerphone, 'You've some questions to answer'. In Russian, of course. OK?"

"We're low on cash."

"Who isn't? Check your post box when you get back."

"Should have said we had a tortoise to feed!" said Sakhno as Nik replaced the receiver. They're happier with animals than they are with humans."

"Who are?"

"The whole damned crowd. How about money?"

"In our box when we get back."

"Bloody nice of them!"

Filling up with petrol on the outskirts of Euskirchen, they took the now familiar road to Trier. Hearing an ambulance siren, Sakhno braked and gave way, but so, too, did the ambulance, signalling vigorously that Sakhno had priority.

"Superstitious clots," muttered Sakhno, driving on.

A setting sun reddened the sky, and although a good hour of daylight remained, the street lights were already on.

At the Trier McDonald's, where they broke for a Big Mac, Nik glanced at one of the newspapers provided for customers and, under Russian Lead in Monschau Murder, read, with growing unease:

Fresh details are to hand concerning the murder of Herr Pogodinsky, proprietor of Masha's Russian restaurant. On two occasions he was visited, shortly before his death, by a balding man of about fifty driving a crimson Jaguar. The man spoke with him at length in Russian, preventing him from attending to other customers. After the man's second visit, Herr Pogodinsky became unwell, and one of the diners summoned an ambulance.

Subsequent to the discovery of Herr Pogodinsky's body, a small 30 × 40 cm. safe was found to be missing from its recess behind a mirror.

Contrary to earlier evidence indicative of suicide, forensic examination now indicates death to have been due to severe trauma affecting liver and kidneys.

The police incline to the view that some time after Herr Pogodinsky's death, bank cards and chequebooks were stolen from the premises. So far, however, no withdrawals have been reported.

"Any gen?" asked Sakhno.

"Nothing special."

Sakhno halted, listened, but there was no sound from the villa.

"Sure there are dogs?"

"Yes."

Two hundred metres along the wall and set some five metres back from it, they found a favourably placed oak tree.

Sakhno listened, then briskly assembled the rifle. Taking aim, he pressed a button on the sight, at which a tiny red circle of light appeared on the bark of the tree. Having hauled himself up, he reached down for the rifle.

"See anything?" Nik called.

"Not yet," responded Sakhno, now high above him.

A long silence followed, broken only by forest rustlings and the distant cry of some night bird.

"Ah, here we are!"

Crack!

"Missed!"

And over the next half hour or so, the crack was repeated.

"Four enough?" Sakhno called.

"I'd say so."

"Coming down."

Sakhno disassembled the rifle, and they made off.

Beyond the wall a door banged, someone shouted.

Sakhno put his foot down and kept it there all the way to Trier, where Nik dialled the number he had been given and left his message.

46

Viktor came back from the Plaza thoroughly disgruntled. Snubbed as *de trop* by the Ukrainian commercial attaché, ignored by Swede and German, after vodka and crab salad he got to his feet, and according his indifferent fellow diners a courteous nod, departed, regretting his order for a chop *à l'argentine*.

On the way to his hotel, he ventured into an ethnic eatery, where, attracting no more attention than the two Negroes and an Arab also present, he enjoyed a microwaved savoury bacon baguette, price three pounds. A bit further on, he came to the pub where he and Wojciech had enjoyed a pint of Murphy's.

Returning to his room, he undressed, and resisting the temptations of the mini-bar, said by Wojciech to be exorbitantly priced, retired to bed and watched TV.

He was woken by a tapping at the door.

"Not locked," he called.

It was Vika.

"Sorry, but the Swede turned amorous. I've only just escaped. Can I lie low here for a bit? Is that the bathroom?"

By the time she emerged he'd got back into his clothes.

"Anything to drink?"

"Try the mini-bar."

She helped herself to Campari and apple juice.

"How about you? Cognac?"

"Why not?"

"You must forgive me," she said with an awkward smile. "Work sometimes involves doing what we'd rather not. Still, better than staying stuck in Kiev."

"What's wrong with Kiev?" he was minded to ask, but didn't.

"I found it just as dull as you did," she continued. "Occasions like that are a bore, but needs must . . . It would be wonderful to stay on here without all that. Or go on to Paris."

Her voice now had something dreamy and romantic about it. He had only to play good listener, but the prospect of seeing her home in an unknown city troubled him.

They watched TV, making further inroads on the mini-bar.

At last Vika got up, as if to visit the bathroom, but was there a long time. Over the TV music, he could hear the shower running.

She returned wrapped in a big towel.

"It's late, and I didn't want you to see me home . . ." she said, slipping into the bed. "Turn off the telly."

He undressed in the dark. Warm hands welcomed him.

"Don't worry. I'm married too!" she whispered.

47

Nik surfaced at 12.30 to a room flooded with bright autumn sunlight, showered and, thinking back over the events of the night, went down to their post box.

A thousand marks. Not a fortune, but enough to be going on with, and setting off for their neighbourhood stores, he returned with two bottles of red, one of Smirnoff, and a quantity of beer.

Sakhno was exercising at the window.

"All's well," said Nik, "there's cash, and I've stocked up with drink."

"To celebrate the shooting season! Good! And for our tortoise?"

Nik felt, and looked, foolish.

"A fine animal lover you are! Back you go. Lettuce. Fresh lettuce. Maybe a cucumber – and what wine did you say?"

"Two of red."

"Get another. And one of those round loaves. We'll charge another mine to departed friends."

The hot German sun made him think of Saratov and its heat. If it came to spending a winter there, as Tanya and Volodya might, they'd have the tiny stove, fashioned by Tanya's metal-worker grandfather. A month's delay at least, he'd said in the telegram for Ivan Lvovich to send, meaning to the end of summer. Now it was autumn, already. Maybe he should write from here. He couldn't explain, only say he was sorry, and they must be patient just a bit longer. Things were, after all, moving to a conclusion. After which, he'd be back in Kiev and could send for them.

Sakhno sniffed Nik's round, small loaf as if it were poisoned.

"Caraway seed!"

"All there was, except for plastic-wrapped sliced."

"God, what they do to bread! Still, let's have some knives and forks," Sakhno said shaking his head, and then, stripping away the outer leaves of the lettuce, called, "Nina, Nina!"

"So you've christened her?"

"I have."

"How do you know it's a she?"

"Shape of tail," Sakhno declared authoritatively, watching Nina crawl purposefully towards the sunlit lettuce.

Sakhno opened the vodka, filled two glasses and fetched sausage from the fridge.

"The dogs! May they rest in peace!"

They clinked glasses and drank.

"Actually," said Nik, "we don't clink glasses at a wake."

"We're not at a wake," said Sakhno, still busy with his mine, "we're relaxing."

Next day, while Sakhno was out sunning Nina on the grass, the phone rang.

"Well?"

"It went OK. Four dogs."

"And you phoned? Splendid. Ring you tomorrow."

Replacing the receiver, Nik wondered what their unseen controllers would make of the newspaper report concerning Pogodinsky.

"Quick!" panted an alarmed Sakhno appearing at the door. "She's run away!"

"Who has?"

"Nina! I was just sitting there, and suddenly, she was gone!"

They raced down the stairs and out into the courtyard.

"She was here."

"She can't have gone far."

Twice they circled the block and were searching under the ornamental shrubs at the base of street lamps, when a little old lady leaned from a window and asked what they were up to.

"We've lost our tortoise," said Nik.

Shutting the window, the old lady came out, and almost at once found Nina behind a litter bin beside the bench Sakhno had been taking his ease on.

While Nik thanked the old lady, Sakhno took Nina up to the flat.

"You must come in for a cup of tea some time," she said. "I don't see much of my son. He's in the police."

48

The last day of the conference saw Vika playing diligent interpreter on the bank processing of dirty money, as if their night together had never been.

At the coffee break, she was smiling intimacy again, but only to ask a favour.

"Could you help by making your number with your Federal Russian colleague, Refat Sibirov, over there?"

"Saying what?"

"You tell him what you're up to, and he'll tell you what he is."

"He won't. We're both bound to official secrecy."

"Still, give it a try," Vika urged. "At least make yourself known to each other for the future."

Viktor stood for a while with his milky coffee, then moved in the direction of Refat who was standing speaking English with two other delegates.

"They're talking English," he said, returning to Vika. "Come and introduce me."

But no sooner were introductions and handshakes completed than the coffee break was over, and they all hurried back to the conference hall.

After the final session Vika dashed off, and Viktor and Wojciech went to a pub, to kill time until the farewell buffet supper at 7.30.

"Learnt anything?" asked Wojciech.

"No," confessed Viktor. "I know damn all about finance. Haven't even got a bank account."

"Re the case you, me and Refat are concerned with, was what I meant."

There must, Viktor saw, drinking beer, be more to Bronitsky's death than met the eye. Something way beyond his own small time inexperience.

"Perhaps we should talk," he said.

"We can. When do you go back?"

"In three days' time."

"I leave the day after tomorrow. Refat flies to Germany tomorrow evening."

"Any idea why?"

"Ask him. Supposing we meet at 1.00 tomorrow in his room?"

"Fine," said Viktor, resolving to say nothing about going to see Bronitsky junior. Getting to Cambridge would be a problem, but Vika would see to that.

No sooner had he changed and was relaxing on his bed than Refat rang.

"Could you come up for a minute?"

He found Refat in a towelling bath robe, fresh from the shower.

"Why the hell set that interpreter woman on me?"

"She insisted. Could be she fancies you."

"More than you?" Refat quipped.

"She did, though. On behalf of the Embassy."

"Interesting." He thought for a moment, then said, "All right, I suppose she's harmless. At least you and I can now chat at the supper this evening. See you here, tomorrow at 1.00."

At the farewell supper, Vita, expensively coiffured and attractively gowned, began by making up to the German from the Plaza dinner, and finished by leaving with Refat.

"Our Moscovy Tartar has all the luck!" sighed Wojciech.

Next day at 1.00 Viktor found Wojciech and Refat studying the menu, and joined Refat in opting for crab soup, vegetable salad and lamb chop with parsley sauce, while Wojciech preferred pork to lamb. Refat phoned through their orders, then poured himself fruit juice. Wojciech produced Polish vodka for Viktor and himself.

"To success!" he said, and they clinked glasses.

"Now," said Refat, looking keenly at Viktor, "it's just a question of our reaching an understanding. Things are moving, and we could get in first, and make a good job of it. It's time we agreed to pool what we know."

"About Bronitsky's killers?"

"Look, let's not play the innocent. It's billions we're after, not killers. They won't bring us any closer to the money."

"Us – how do you mean?" The sum was as astonishing as the fact of being made privy to it.

"That can wait, but there'll be no cause for complaint."

A waiter knocked, wheeled in a trolley, served them, and went out.

For a while they ate in silence. Then, after suitably recharging all their glasses, Wojciech raised his to Viktor.

"Well?"

Smiling, Viktor raised his glass to Wojciech.

"Right then," said Refat, "here's something more for you. One of those tailing our two fugitives to the German frontier was Captain Kylimnik, Ukrainian Border Troops, presently at Border Troops HQ. A year back he was taken off the Ukraino-Russian Frontier Delimitation Commission. Why, we don't know. You could find out more easily in Kiev. He'd once been on good terms with Bronitsky."

Useful stuff, something to go on, except that he'd have to sift what and what not to pass on to Georgiy. Keeping Refat and Wojciech out of the picture wouldn't be easy, even supposing, as was by no means certain, that their co-operation was genuine.

49

Nik slept badly, his head muzzy from Sakhno's cannabis, his mind racing with the need to shoot dogs and ring 546-33. He went for a drink of water, and on his way back noticed the carrier bag with Pogodinsky's notebooks. Struck by a sudden thought, he took one of them over to the window, where, by the light of the street lamp, he saw that 546-33 was Weinberg's number. His, then, were the dogs they had thrown fish to and shot. A wealthy man, on the face of it, connected with Pogodinsky in some way, and still driving the crimson Jaguar which the police were looking for.

Was it Weinberg who had murdered Pogodinsky?

Nik and Sakhno's rôle had been purely and simply to rattle the bars of Weinberg's cage, frighten and unsettle him into betraying some lead, possibly to the money Ivan Lvovich had spoken of.

He seemed suddenly to see what the link might be between the opulent Weinberg behind his two-metre wall and the wretched Pogodinsky, restaurateur, chef, waiter, dishwasher all in one, living above tiny premises. Weinberg would have been the Cashier, to whom Pogodinsky would have paid a percentage of profits – until the break up of the Soviet Union. Told, six years later, to make good arrears, he'd been unable to. Weinberg's visits would have been to put the squeeze on, rather than murder and string the man up. That would have been someone else's handiwork.

The man who phoned gave no why or wherefore for his instructions. Why? Security reasons? Or because, being disposable, he and Sakhno had no need to know?

Emerging from the shower, Sakhno drank the coffee Nik had ready, and asked for another.

"Weren't you going to give me some money?"

"What money?"

"My half of what was sent."

"Actually, no."

"Let's have five hundred, then."

"Don't I get something towards the cost of food?"

"We'll sort that out. Come on."

Nik handed him five hundred-mark notes.

Sakhno dressed slowly, and drank a glass of water.

"Back tonight," he said, and left.

Nik went back to bed, and slept.

In the clear-headedness of waking, he saw the folly of giving Sakhno so large a sum of money, against which had to be set the satisfaction of being rid of him for a while.

He showered. It was 2.30. He put fresh lettuce down for Nina, he dressed, and went out.

As he stood in the square, taking in church, chemists, cafés, Norma supermarket and a butcher's, a bus drew up, the door opened and the driver waited for him to board.

Nik shook his head. The bus moved off. Someone waved. He waved back. It was the little old lady who had helped to find Nina.

Discovering a pleasant café, he treated himself to a coffee and a white fruit-fudge mouse.

Then he proceeded through a light warm drizzle to the post office, bought an envelope, paper and stamps for Russia, and standing at a high table, wrote:

My dear Tanya and Volodya,

I keep wondering how you are, what you're doing, whether you're cold at the dacha. Things are dragging a bit, but I'm sure another month or two will see us reunited in Kiev. I'm fine, but travelling Europe. Interesting, but dull without you. One day we'll both come to this café where I've just had coffee and tried German fruit fudge.

If it gets really cold, borrow from your people and rent a flat. I'll send money just as soon as I can.

With love, kisses and best wishes to all, Nik.

He sighed and crossed out the bit about sending money. Much as he wanted, he couldn't send money to Saratov from here. He addressed the envelope, sealed it, \ and licked the stamp, overlooking the damp pad provided.

Leaving the post office and the yellow post box in the wall outside, he walked, through a steady drizzle, past other boxes, reluctant to post what he knew he should not have written.

At last, too sodden to post, the letter slipped from his fingers, and he let it lie.

50

Taking off from Gatwick, Viktor felt weary, puzzled, disappointed. He'd soon be back in Kiev in his office. Georgiy would want to be told the next to nothing Viktor had to tell, while having vastly more to tell him.

With the help of a travel bureau where they spoke Russian, he'd made his own way to Cambridge, and had no sooner stepped from the train, than he came across two young women speaking Russian, who, being at the language school he sought, kindly took him there and translated for him.

Bronitsky, it emerged, had been collected by Embassy car. Something to do with his mother had made it necessary for him immediately to fly back to Kiev.

Thanking his young helpers, Viktor returned to his London hotel and rang Vika.

The Embassy knew nothing of Bronitsky. What he'd been told in Cambridge had no basis in reality. The Embassy possessed only two cars and they were in constant use. In circumstances such as he described, the Embassy would simply telephone or write. It was no part of Embassy duties to put people on planes to Kiev. The young man might well have been collected by a personal courier service.

The in-flight lunch did much to improve Viktor's mood. As to Bronitsky junior, God alone knew what had happened, but in Kiev so would he. In an hour or two Georgiy would be ringing, and he must think out what to tell him. Wojciech's photographs, safe in his breast pocket, inspired for the moment a sense of his own superior worth. For once, he, Viktor, was one up on the invariably better informed Georgiy, and he smiled at the thought.

51

Next morning, Sakhno stood for a while at the window enjoying the warm autumn sun, then dressed, and without a word to Nik went out, taking Nina with him. Nik saw him sit on the bench, putting Nina beside his feet on the grass.

She'll wander off again, he thought, putting the kettle on the stove. He made himself coffee and took another look out of the window. Sakhno was still sitting on the bench, bent forward, eyes fixed on Nina, immobile on the grass in the sun.

He had time to breakfast and shave before Sakhno came back, looking more his old self, and cut thin slices of cucumber, which he arranged around the edge of a saucer, slightly over-hanging it.

"To give her a change from lettuce," he explained. "Can you lend me two hundred?"

"Shall I ever get it back?"

"Yes."

Without a word he pocketed the money, picked up the case containing the rifle, and let himself out.

"What's that for?" Nik called, dashing after him.

"No need to shout. Back this evening," came the reply.

Nik decided to repeat his walk of the day before, leaving the flat empty, except, of course, for Nina, who would ignore the phone, were it to ring with further unwelcome instructions.

Over coffee and a fudge mouse, he wondered at the number of chemists he could see from the window. Maybe there was a lot of sickness. On the other hand, maybe people were living longer and needing tablets and vitamins.

The little old lady who had helped to find Nina appeared, pulling a shopping trolley. Seeing Nik, she waved, parked her trolley outside the café, and came in.

"Hello, young man," she smiled. "How's your tortoise?"

"Fine."

"Not been here long, have you? How do you like it?"

"It's a nice town."

"Like to join me in a bite to eat? Keep me company? I never see much of my son. It's cabbage soup."

Nik thanked her.

"12.30, then. Flat 3."

Nik presented himself at Flat 3 with an offering of supermarket gateau.

"Your phone's been ringing," she said. "Such thin walls. Building's not what it was before the war."

Her flat was just like theirs, but better furnished.

"I can hear you moving about, you know," she said, pointing to the ceiling. "And when I'm in the bath and your phone goes, I think it's mine. Except that nobody rings me, except for the doctor and my son. Where are you from?"

"The Volga."

"A *Volksdeutscher*, then. Well, let's eat."

The soup was indeed cabbage, and nothing else, apart from potato.

As the little old lady served the gateau, Nik's telephone began to ring.

"Off you go, there'll be tea when you come back," she said, opening the door.

Nik took his time, but the phone was still ringing when he got there.

"Taken short or something? Where've you been?"

"I was out."

"So I gathered. Now listen carefully. Today you ring 546-33 three times from the flat. Prefix 0450. 'Coming with questions the day after tomorrow,' is the recorded message you leave. Make the first call now, the next at 6.00, then one at 10.00. Tomorrow you ring five times saying, 'Correction: not tomorrow, today.' "

"What if he answers before the machine?"

"Tell him you'll ring back and ring me on 48-04. Got it? Call you tomorrow evening."

Nik drank tea, ate a slice of gateau with the little old lady, thanked her, and returned to his flat to ring Trier.

52

During Viktor's brief time in England, autumn had come to Kiev. Red leaves, yellow leaves crackled underfoot. Warmer clothes were the order. Bright sun was offset by an icy wind.

Zanozin met him at the airport in the Mazda, and as they headed along the Borisopol Highway, Viktor's mobile rang.

"Welcome back! Not alone, I take it."

"Correct."

"And heading for home?"

"Correct."

"Ring you in forty minutes."

Viktor turned to Zanozin. "What's been happening?"

"Next to nothing as regards Bronitsky. But a cull of Assembly candidates seems to have started. Two murdered in Kiev, one in Simferopol, one in Dnepropetrovsk – all in the same week."

"Not our pigeon."

"Except that District may have to take on responsibility for the security of certain candidates, so General Voronov said at an Internal Affairs Ministry conference. 'Certain candidates' being those put forward by the Ministry."

"Take the car back to Division, I'll make my own way," Viktor said, getting out outside his block and retrieving his bag from the back seat. "I'll be there in two hours' time, tell the Major."

He watched the Mazda drive slowly away.

The flat was clean and bright, as if to welcome his return, and Ira was pleased to see him.

"Have a wash and come and eat."

"Where's Yana?"

"Asleep."

He tucked into the meat dumplings with relish, filled with an optimism only partly to do with the bright sun. Success was within his grasp. Those photographs bade fair to lead to those whose admissions would set the seal on the Bronitsky affair. He could now out-trump even Georgiy.

"What are you smiling about?" asked Ira.

"Just thinking."

"Of Yana's birthday, for instance?"

"But it isn't."

"To the age of one she has a birthday every month."

"So?"

"Have you got her a present?"

For Ira he'd bought a £20 set of toiletries in the Gatwick Duty-

Free, after seeing what a young woman bought for herself.

"I'm afraid not."

"Don't worry, we'll get her something here. More dumplings?"

As they were drinking coffee his mobile rang.

"Nice shower?"

"And a nice meal."

"The news is that Widow Bronitsky died this morning."

Ira crept from the room, taking her coffee with her.

"Knocked down walking home. No witnesses. What about the son?"

"Collected from the school three days ago in an Embassy car. Needed back in Kiev. Something had happened to his mother. The Embassy disclaims all knowledge."

"And as regards the mother, a curious time lag between us and England. So you had a wasted journey?"

"Not entirely. We had lectures on mafia money-laundering, and I've a list of suspect banks."

"You met colleagues from other countries, I suppose."

"I did."

"Well, off you go and see if District's got anything further about the Widow. Call you this evening."

Slipping a pack of Caffrey's Irish Ale into a carrier bag for Ratko, he set off for District, telling Ira he'd be back in three or four hours.

Seeing no sign of his Mazda, he asked the guard if he knew what Zanozin was up to.

"Not yet back from the airport," said the guard.

"You've been in great demand," said Ratty, concealing the Irish Ale under his desk. "Ministry kept ringing, Directorate kept ringing and somewhere else rang too. Ten calls at least. All asking when you'd be back. Back today, I said, but so far today no one's rung."

Returning to his office, more than a little irritated at the non-return of his Mazda, Viktor fetched the Bronitsky file from his safe, and spread the recent photographs on the desk before him. He'd give Zanozin a rocket for joyriding, then tell him to get details of the Widow's death and the home address of Border Troops Captain Kylimnik.

The door banged open.

"He's in intensive care, your Zanozin!" announced Ratko. "Rocket launcher attack at the South Bridge approach."

"Have we a car?"

"Take the Zhiguli. You'll find Kharkov District in attendance."

"When did it happen?"

"Two hours ago."

"Why the delay?"

"Took time to identify the driver."

Pausing only to lock file and photographs in the safe, Viktor rushed out to the Zhiguli.

53

By the time Nik made his final phone call, Sakhno had still not returned.

Supposing he didn't return – what then?

His thoughts turned to Weinberg's dogs. Next it would be some person or persons who would have to be shot.

The phone rang.

"How's your pal?"

"Fine. Gone for a drive."

"His last for a bit. Ring tomorrow, as I said, and call me if they answer. Keep your friend off drink and the other, and see he gets a good night's sleep. Your next trip's the day after tomorrow."

The "last for a bit" had a disturbingly ominous ring.

Nina having long since retired beneath the radiator, Nik too went to bed.

Next morning, Sakhno had still not returned.

Nik drank coffee, made the phone call, shopped in the supermarket, and visiting his café, was alarmed to hear talk of a collision somewhere in the vicinity between a bus and another vehicle at 8.30 that morning.

Hurrying back to the flat, he put down lettuce and cucumber for Nina. It was getting on for 11.00, time for his second phone call. Suddenly he heard the familiar sound of the hearse, and rushing to the window, saw it turning in to park behind the house.

Sakhno came in empty-handed, without the rifle case.

"Where on earth have you been?"

"Why the old-womanly concern?" he asked, pulling out a wad of notes. "And here's your seven hundred back."

"And the rifle?"

"In the hearse. Didn't know you wanted to go shooting."

"Well, go and fetch it."

"Go yourself." He threw over the keys. "And you can stop being bossy. I, too, bring in the money!"

He flourished his wad of notes.

"You do realize that the police are onto us," Nik said evenly.

"Where did you get that from?"

"The paper that's still in the car. If you like to fetch it, I'll translate." He threw the keys back. "And bring the rifle."

While Sakhno was gone, Nik made his call.

The newspaper report left Sakhno unimpressed.

"That's about burglars, not us."

"It will be, if they look hard enough. Come and have some tea. It's Trier again tomorrow."

Sakhno made a face.

"What's wrong?"

"One, I'm out of bullets and so can't shoot. Two, I'm brassed off with working for damn all!"

54

For three days Zanozin lay in a coma, and Viktor visited the military hospital several times each day.

It was still too early to say how good a chance he had. His lungs were clear of blood, but he still had metal in his chest, and was in danger of heart failure.

"May I see him?"

"Just for a minute."

Zanozin was all bandages and projecting tubes. His eyes were shut.

As Viktor stood at the bedside, assailed by feelings of guilt and a sense of responsibility, his mobile rang, and he retreated to the corridor.

"How is he?"

"Still in a coma."

"I've a nasty feeling there's something you've not told me."

"How so?"

"The logic of it. You go to England, someone here tries to kill you. You're lucky it's not you lying there in a coma. You must be onto something? So come on, tell me what."

"Can we speak this evening?"

"I'll call at 7.00."

On his way back to District, Viktor dropped into McDonald's for a cheeseburger and coffee, and staring out at a steady drizzle, thought suddenly of Dima Rakin of Special Branch F., who had got him into all this, and rang him.

"No longer with us," was the chilly response.

"Where can I find him?"

"What's your connection?"

"We were MVD together."

"OK. Baykov Cemetery, Plot 64, is where you'll find him."

"You mean, he's dead?"

"Rush hour accident. Fell under a train. Obolon metro station."

At 7.00 Viktor sat on in his office. It was dark outside, and raining. The hospital reported no change.

At last Georgiy rang.

"Well? What have you got?"

"Photos."

"Where are you at the moment?"

"District."

"The photos too? Right. October Palace, Exhibition Hall construction site entrance. You'll see two hooded back-to-back public phones. Be there thirty minutes from now."

Viktor eyed the SVI duty groundsheet-cape on its wooden peg in the corner. There were no umbrellas. Just as well. "The cop with a brolly ends up on a trolley," was one of Ratko's pearls of wisdom. So he would go as groundsheet-caped SVI man.

Viktor stood under the phone hood out of the rain, wondering where Georgiy would appear from, when Georgiy spoke from the other side of the partition.

"Stay where you are – we can talk like this. Let's have the photos."

Viktor passed the envelope under the partition.

"Tell me about them."

"The two men in denim suits hopped it from Kiev the day after Bronitsky died. The other two tailed them from Poland to the German frontier. The close-cropped one is Captain Kylimnik of Border Troops HQ."

"Good lad," said Georgiy, rather to Viktor's surprise. "Where did you get them?"

"Our Polish equivalent. Otherwise confidential."

"So be it. Just so long as the result of your investigation isn't also confidential! Next step?"

"To tackle Kylimnik," said Viktor, caught unawares by the question.

"Leave Kylimnik to me."

"Isn't this where we came in?" Viktor exploded. "I'm the one investigating and damned near getting killed in the process!"

"Let's put it this way," soothed Georgiy, "I'm director, you're official executive."

"And official *target*?"

"True, but under my protection, which is good against most things. If we win, you get the medals, I stay in the background. OK? The endgame's where bodies mount, remember, so take care not to be one of them. How are you getting home?"

"By metro."

"No. Go back to District and take the duty car. Ring you tomorrow morning. I'll return the photos."

"How am I to cope without an aide?"

"Leave that with me."

Looking back, as he walked away, he caught sight of Georgiy disappearing into the rainy darkness. Taller, more heavily built than Viktor, he wore a long cape, his top half concealed by his umbrella.

55

Sakhno rose at 9.00 next morning, put lettuce and sliced cucumber down for Nina, and taking the rifle case, left, closing the door quietly behind him, as if out of consideration for Nik.

But far from asleep, Nik lay reconciled to the fact that no intervention on his part would have changed Sakhno's plans in the slightest, or improved his own state of mind.

He returned to the flat from a walk in the rain to find the phone ringing.

"Change of plan," said the man. "Set off nearer 6.00 and get there before dark. Kick up a racket, bring the guards out, and your friend opens fire. If he wings or bags anyone, so much the better. Phone from Trier on the way back, and say, 'Pierre agrees to talk in two days time.' Got that? Call you tomorrow."

6.00 came and went. Nik took a beer from the fridge, and went over to the open window. The moist, refreshing evening air induced a feeling of calm, suspended thought. He raised the bottle to his lips. He no longer gave a damn.

Next morning it was still raining, and there was still no sign of Sakhno. Perhaps he was never coming back. Nik stared at Nina as if she was empowered to answer for him.

At 10.00, when the phone rang, Nik explained the position.

"Ring you back," said the man, after a lengthy silence.

When he did, his voice was muted.

"Stay by the phone. An old friend's going to give you a call."

Nik made tea, took it over to the open window, and by the time the phone rang, had again achieved a state of total indifference.

"Nik, it's me, Ivan Lvovich."

"Where are you?"

"In far-off Kiev. And with some bad news . . . I don't know how to tell you . . . It's your wife, Nik, and your son – they're dead."

Nik stood transfixed.

"What – what did you say?"

"Nik, I'm terribly, terribly sorry. There was a fire. Maybe the stove got overstoked. Look, we'll get you back in a day or two. Forget all the rest. We'll ring. Be brave, Nik."

56

For two more days Zanozin's condition remained unchanged, and the doctor did not hold out much hope. Zanozin's youthful mother had arrived from Sumy, and Ratko was cheered by her presence. Every day he had brought oranges for the patient, which, to his annoyance, daily disappeared. "What patients don't eat, the nurses take," a doctor had explained. Now Mrs Zanozin took the oranges, keeping them in a carrier bag in the bedside table, where, as she confided to Viktor, blushing with embarrassment, there was now any number of oranges, some going bad.

Viktor, who till then had come empty-handed, took the hint, and next time brought half a sausage and a fresh black loaf, for which Mrs Zanozin was very grateful.

"I can understand the nurses doing what they do," she said. "Sixty a month is all they get, and you can't live on that. No wonder they don't make much effort."

"And how much do you get?"

"The pension, which, as you know, is 49.90, and never gets paid on time. Still, there's one nice nurse here who brings me tea."

"First-rate, those photos," said Georgiy, ringing Viktor at District. "We've made two more identifications. The chap with Kylimnik is Vasily Portnov, also known as Port. Served with Special Forces. Two convictions since. In the other photo we have Sergey Sakhno, also known as Sapper. He was one once. He's done dirty jobs for Security. Not overbright. Neurasthenic. Uses drugs. Exported 'for disposal' would be my reading for him. But his companion we've not been able to identify. Still, I think I get the picture."

"Which is?"

"That Sakhno and his companion were being shadowed to prevent their doubling back to Ukraine. Sakhno will have been given the chop in Germany, and by now his companion too. Professional requirement. It's ninety-nine per cent certain that both pairs are, were, directly linked with the Bronitsky business."

"Where are the other two now?"

"Portnov's disappeared. Unconfirmed reports say to Russia. Kylimnik is currently Assistant Military Attaché at our Embassy in Paris."

"Since when?"

"The last two weeks."

"So do I go to Paris?"

"You may well have to. Give me a couple of days. I'll float the idea. But watch it. If he's big time, this Kylimnik, you won't even make the plane. If he isn't, he'll get run over in Paris."

"But if he doesn't, and I don't go under a train on the metro?"

"In that case, no security leak. Get it? So give me time. No packing, no talk of Eiffel Towers! Not yet. Suss out Border Troops HQ, that's the next job.

"So for the next few days, you take the duty car, park, at noon precisely, at the Cavalry Street–Vladimir Street junction, observe comings and goings for the next thirty minutes, then buzz off."

"Looking for what?"

"Just keeping an eye on the door."

Viktor collected an unstamped envelope and some junk mail from their post box, and took the new lift up to their flat. Ira and Yana were already in bed. Quietly, he shut himself into the kitchen and sat down at the table.

The envelope contained the message, "In Kiev tomorrow. Meet you 10 p.m., Hydropark metro station, Lisova line platform. Refat."

A curious rendezvous, and not one he was mentally prepared for. He had, since their London agreement to pool information, learnt things which, if communicated, would show him to be the source of the leak. Still, without Refat and his photos, Georgiy would not have made his identifications. So, purely and simply for the good of the investigation, and in the hope of some return . . . Albeit with a nasty premonition of one day finding himself written off for collaborating with "the Russian enemy".

The Georgiy-inspired watch on Border Troops HQ produced little of note beyond that, of the men passing in and out, none were in uniform, whereas at the Zolotovorotsky Lane entrance Georgiy had expressed no interest in, all were, their parked cars being of a poorer order.

Returning to District, he learnt that a drunken caretaker claimed, belatedly, to have seen a young man shove Widow Bronitsky into the path of an old white Mercedes, but that, interrogated further, he had been unable to remember either the make or colour of the vehicle.

Leaving the duty Zhiguli at Arsenal, Viktor took the metro to Hydropark, and at 9.57 was the only one to alight there. A train came in from the opposite direction, opened and closed its doors, and continued on its way.

"Greetings," came a familiar voice, and there, from nowhere, was Refat, in elegant, knee-length raincoat and carrying an umbrella.

Keeping to unlit paths, they made their way into Hydropark, and Viktor told Refat who was who in the photographs, and of the fate of Widow Bronitsky.

"What about the son you saw in England?"

"I didn't. He'd been collected by the Embassy and put on a plane, his mother having been involved in an accident."

"As indeed she was, but later."

"So you know."

"No, not entirely. How could we? Is that the lot?"

"Yes."

"My contribution is the fourth man. We'll know for certain in a couple of days, but if we're right, he's a military interpreter. Left

Dushanbe for Kiev on the say-so of a certain Kiev colonel, sending wife and son to relatives in Saratov – while he got settled and looked for a flat – their effects having been sent to Kiev in advance. Wife and son sit expecting to hear. Two months pass, then out of the blue comes a letter from someone here saying our interpreter's left money with him for safe keeping, and as he hasn't returned, what should he do with it?"

"Is there any way of establishing if that's him?"

"A man's gone to Saratov with the photographs. If it is the husband, there'll be the problem of keeping the wife and the son quiet for a bit. Red Cross Missing Person inquiries are the last thing we want. It would be good to get hold of the colonel who enticed him into coming to Kiev."

The eerie silence of Hydropark was broken by a sudden patter of rain on foliage invisible in the dark. Refat opened his umbrella over them both.

Seeing a figure stretched on a bench, Viktor stopped abruptly.

"Drunk or dead," said Refat. "Come on."

But Viktor still stood as if in a different world.

Refat came and bent over the man.

"Drunk," he said straightening. "Roughed up and robbed. Come on, he won't die of cold."

They went on deeper into the park, which, at that hour, had all the air of a sinister forest.

"I've got a couple more days here," said Refat as they headed back towards the lights. "If there's any news, you'll get a letter."

57

Well into a second bottle of Absolut, Nik sat by the window gazing out at the rain.

He began, for the first time, to feel genuine pity for Sakhno, whose pregnant fiancée had been knocked down and killed by a car. Whether or not by accident, was no longer of such consequence as the fact of death itself.

He'd given no thought to what had caused the fire that had killed Tanya and Volodya, accepting it as an accident. Grandfather's little stove was old, but perfectly safe if properly tended.

He and Sakhno were in the same boat. No longer anybody's now their nearest and dearest were dead. Like lost dogs.

Lost, despite still having masters and food. There was no sense to anything – going on included.

This promise "to get him back" – back where? Dushanbe? Saratov? Kiev? Home? He had no home.

Collapsing onto his bed, he slept until woken by the phone.

"Your pal not back?"

"No. When do I get away?"

"You must wait, you can't just leave him."

"He's not coming back."

"He's got nowhere else to go. Just hang on. When he does come, give him two of the tablets, and get your things together."

So that was it!

"Still there? I've put today's paper in your post box. You'll see the score. Ring when he's had the tablets, and we'll come and get you."

Nina's water dish was empty. Nik refilled it, cleared away the old lettuce and uneaten cucumber, and put down fresh.

He no longer wanted Sakhno to come back. Not to be given tablets and die.

The fridge was empty apart from three cans of beer. He had just two hundred DM left.

At the local shop he bought two tins of haricot soup, bread and sausage, and on his way back to the flat collected the newspaper from their post box.

MAFIA WAR HITS KOBLENZ STREETS ran the headline.

Ferencs Szabo, Hungarian procurer of girls from Eastern Europe for illegal brothels in North Rhine Westphalia, was last night shot dead near the Bismarck Monument. Szabo, according to police sources, had recently attempted to seize control of the contraband cigarette trade, traditionally the province of the deaf-and-dumb community. Szabo's German girlfriend and two of his bodyguards died last year in clashes with the Russian Mafia. Eyewitnesses state that Szabo was shot by a man aged about forty from a hearse driven by a young blonde. Anyone with information concerning this incident should contact the Koblenz Police.

Nik reached for the bottle of Absolut. No, Sakhno would not be back now.

58

Viktor's second watch on the entrance of Border Troops HQ proved more rewarding than the first. No sooner had he taken up position than a man in a leather jacket tapped on his window.

"Waiting for somebody?"

"Yes," said Viktor, lowering it.

A little later he noticed movement at a first floor window. The curtain moved aside and two men looked out, one of them very like the man in the leather jacket.

In the course of the next half hour he was subjected to three inspections from the same window.

Zanozin was still on a ventilator and in a coma.

"How is he?" Viktor asked Mrs Zanozin, depositing a carrier bag containing sausage, cheese and a carton of apple juice on the bedside table.

"No change, the doctor says. And if after three days there's still no change, that's it. This ward's only got the one ventilator."

"Have something to eat," he said passing her the bag.

She thanked him warmly.

"If he'd been a State Deputy or a General, my poor Misha, they'd have whisked him off to Germany or Austria and saved his life, so one of the nurses said."

That evening Georgiy rang.

"What news of our HQ?"

"They're beginning to keep an eye on me."

"Splendid! Tomorrow could be interesting. I'll ring. Oh, and you'll find those photos back in your safe."

No plodding through rain, no slipping under a partition for Georgiy!

Viktor's third watch passed uneventfully, but driving away from Border Troops HQ, he was tailgated and twice rammed by a green 4 × 4, as if to force him into the path of oncoming traffic. Point made, the 4 × 4 dropped back.

Back at District Viktor sat, not in the best of moods, watching the sun gain ascendency over cloud, when Refat rang.

"How far to Koncha-on-the-Lakes?"

"Twenty minutes."

"So off you go. House 28 – no street name – Tarnavsky, Valentin. He's the one who wrote to Saratov. Show him the photos, see if he gives us our fourth man."

"Bit of a comedown after the Mazda, eh?" remarked the guard as Viktor made for the duty Zhiguli.

"It goes."

All the way to Koncha-on-the-Lakes he was tailed by a cherry-red Samara, which, when he stopped in the writers' village, drove on past.

Tarnavsky, at 2.00 in the afternoon, had clearly only just got out of bed. The kitchen where they sat had no clock, and the whole place had an air of time suspended.

"You wrote to a lady in Saratov about a sum of money left with you by her husband," Viktor began.

"I did. Are you from her?"

"I'm not." Viktor produced his envelope of photographs. "But I'd like you to look at these and tell me if one of the men is him."

"Yes, that's Nik," he said pointing him out. "Nice chap."

Having elicited from Tarnavsky as much as he could remember, Viktor rose to go.

"This money, what do I do with it?"

"If you give me your number, I'll ring."

The cherry-red Samara tailed him all the way back to Kiev. He noted its registration number. At least it had the decency not to ram him.

59

The next two days were a protracted nightmare. His money was nearly finished and so, it seemed, was his life. The phone rang and he let it ring, at first not wanting to answer, but later not able to. Five empty bottles of Absolut littered the floor beneath the table. Staggering in a haze to the table, he seemed to see Tanya and Volodya waving, calling.

After two more glasses, he took a sheet of paper and wrote: "They want you dead. Hop it. Koblenz cops onto the hearse. Ditch it. Best of luck, Nik."

He poured the last of his vodka into a cup, added two of Ivan Lvovich's tablets, watched them effervesce, then gulped the mixture down.

60

Viktor's fourth watch on Border Troops HQ passed uneventfully except for the arrival in the last few minutes of a stretch Chrysler. Two close-cropped giants got out and looked around before opening the rear door for a thin man in a long, tight-fitting overcoat who went quickly into the HQ building. Viktor wrote down the registration number, then saw that he was himself under observation from the second floor.

He pressed the starter, circled the flower bed in front of the main entrance, and was heading for the T-junction with Vladimir Street when an enormous lorry came bouncing over the cobbles towards him. He braked, intending to reverse out of trouble, but in the panic of the moment engaged first gear.

When at last he opened his eyes, he saw Ratko.

"I thought I heard my wife."

"I met her coming out as I came in," said Ratko. "Don't worry – you're only here for a couple of days. You were bloody lucky, the doctor says. And the safety belt helped. Damn all left of the car, though."

"How about Zanozin?"

"Off the ventilator. Breathing normally."

"What's the score with me?"

"Broken leg. Concussion. Soon be your old self and back on the waiting list. You'll have your three-roomer in time for your daughter's wedding."

Viktor smiled.

"That's an old one! What happened to the lorry?"

"Nothing much. Made of tougher stuff than your car. Brakes failed. Driver messed his face up going through the screen. We'll mess it up a bit more when he's better! Driving in the city centre with deficient brakes!"

Ratko went his way, leaving a bag of oranges and Viktor with his right leg in plaster and strung up in the air.

61

Nik spent the night vomiting, suffering attacks of diarrhoea, and longing for death that seemed so slow in coming. But it was not until dawn that he finally collapsed senseless onto the floor beside his bed.

The door latch clicked, followed by footsteps, not so much heard as felt through the floor, then two blurry silhouettes stood over him.

"Always knew you were the dotty one," came Sakhno's voice. "Hanging or shooting's better than poisoning, and more reliable – especially when the poison's a super-fast laxative! Here, drink this."

It was the last beer from the fridge, and it did something to assuage the Sahara-like aridity of his mouth. Cups of tea completed the cure, he was able to sit up, become aware of the young blonde female with Sakhno, and the fact that they were conversing in deaf-and-dumb language.

"So now we're quits," said Sakhno. "Though I deserve extra special for swapping the tablets."

"When was that?" Nik managed to ask.

"Back in Belarus. I had some for you. They were given to me in Kiev."

"I don't get it."

"No mystery. We do the job, one of us gets told to kill the other, after which, what simpler than to give him the chop."

"When exactly did you hit on that?"

"The moment they gave me the tablets and said you'd be in a denim suit like mine."

Nik fell back and lay staring at the ceiling, while Sakhno and the girl stood conversing by the stove.

"What's your friend's name?"

"Uli, Ulrike."

"Pretty . . . So that was you two in Koblenz."

"Where did you get that from?"

"The man who phones left a newspaper. It's there somewhere."

Sakhno found it and Nik translated.

"And that's why you decided to opt out?"

"No. I'd just heard that my wife and son had died in a fire. It was after that I was told to look for the paper. And when you got back, you were to be given the tablets."

Sakhno looked at him with new interest. "So you decided not to wait for me."

"It's all over. No sense to anything. They'd get me back, they said. But back where?"

"It's bloody well not all over! We're only just starting!"

"You and Uli are wanted by the police, I'm a dead loss – what the hell can we start?"

"What about the money?"

"What money?"

"The money we were to find, then be killed for finding. We're nearly there, man! All we have to do is go to Trier and shake the tree."

"Money's no use to me."

"So, I'll have your share. And actually we don't need to go to Trier. This chap who phones is who we want, and he'll be somewhere in this one-eyed town. Any ideas?"

"I've got his telephone number. His address can be got by working through the directory."

"So we go for the money?"

"You do."

"We both do. I need you to speak German."

While Sakhno busied himself with the directory and Uli fussed over Nina, Nik fell asleep.

62

With Zanozin and Viktor on different floors in the same hospital, Ratko was able, as he put it, "to kill two hares with the same bullet". Viktor did his best to do justice to the constant supply of oranges, and Ira helped. Even so, they made little impression on it.

The first snow fell. No longer was his leg suspended from the crane-like device, and the day came when he was issued with crutches, for which he signed, and taken by ambulance to Kharkovsky and his flat to mobilize and resume normal life.

"How long are you laid up for?" Georgiy inquired.

"The plaster comes off in three weeks."

"Sounds grim. Still, the driver of the lorry's hanged himself. 'Overcome with remorse.' I don't think!"

"Don't think what?"

"That *he* hanged *himself*. What came as a surprise was that you were being photographed from the windows of State Security opposite, as well as observed from HQ."

"How do you know?"

"You were watching the doors, we were watching for reaction. So you've stirred up two ministries by the look of it. State Security's drawn your file from Personnel."

"So what do I do?"

"Nothing, just get better. Let events take their course without you. Safer that way. I'll keep you in touch."

Outside it was dark, but it was no longer snowing. Autumn was slowly giving way to winter.

63

"Up you get," Sakhno urged, rousing Nik from an uneasy half sleep. "I've got the address."

"What time is it?"

"4.00."

"Can't it wait till morning?"

"Look, while you've been blissfully sleeping, I have spent hours going through the phone book!"

Heaving himself to his feet, Nik saw that Sakhno's bed had been taken over by Uli.

"48-04 is Überkraft, N., Schönparkallee, 18. And that's here," Sakhno pointed to the top left corner of the street map in the directory.

"What are you going to do?"

"Pay him a visit."

"And then?"

"Like you said, make a run for it."

Their footsteps rang out loud and crisp in the silence of the sleeping town, until snow began to fall, steadily muffling them.

Schönparkallee, 18, proved to be a bungalow set back behind a low, well-trimmed hedge.

Sakhno led Nik round to the back, where they found a vent of the kitchen window open.

"Give me a leg up," he whispered, and by the time Nik joined him, had beer, sausage and cheese ready in the light of the open fridge.

"We'll breakfast first, in case there's no time later. I like eating out. And there's a bottle of Stolichnaya in the fridge that leaves with us when we go."

"Time we met our host," Sakhno said, taking a kitchen knife and marching off into the darkness.

Sakhno was now leader. Nik was content to be led.

Following more slowly, he found Sakhno, in a blaze of light, holding the knife to the throat of a bewildered Überkraft still snug in bed.

Physically persuaded by Sakhno, Überkraft finally responded to questioning in Russian.

"It was me delivered the rifle. I collected it from left luggage, Cologne station."

"Who told you to ring and what to do?"

"Medvedev. My controller in Soviet days. After the break-up, total silence. But two months ago, he phones, tells me I'm reactivated. Tells me to take you under my wing, find you a flat."

Weinberg, so far as he knew, was a disaffected former agent, with high-level contacts and high-level involvements. Hence the order to call him to account. It was all money, money, money, today. Ideology was out.

"Why did we have to frighten up Pogodinsky?" Nik asked.

"Question of money. He hadn't paid the interest."

"On what?"

"The restaurant. It wasn't his. It was financed by the Committee."

"Who was he to pay the interest to?"

"Weinberg, I think. He'd been to see Pogodinsky before we took over."

They left Überkraft trussed but ungagged.

Outside it was still snowing.

64

After only three days, Viktor was bored to tears, and irritated at Ira's undisguised pleasure at having him confined to the flat.

"You should break your leg more often," she told him.

One evening, when Ira was busy putting Yana to bed, the bell rang, and hobbling as fast as he could on his crutches, he managed to catch the postman before he returned to the lift.

"Special Delivery. From Moscow. Sign here, please."

He signed, and hobbled back to the kitchen.

The envelope contained a typed but unsigned letter, presumably from Refat, and the photostat copy of a handwritten letter. The former read:

> Our fourth man was at Euskirchen, near Cologne. The enclosed, together with envelope addressed to wife and son, seems to have been dropped in the mud and cleaned up afterwards. My guess is that it was posted to create the impression that our friend was still alive, he having been prevented from posting it himself. Amateurish and a bit of a puzzle.

Looking at Tsensky in the photograph, Viktor felt sorry for his having to write home so impersonally.

Taking his tea over to the window, he pressed his face to the glass.

Parked at the block entrance, cab light on, was a minivan. A car drew up. A man got out, and the minivan moved off in the direction of the metro and the Kharkov Highway.

65

"Belgium next, so get the map," Sakhno informed Nik, sitting squeezed against Uli on the front seat of the hearse. Uli was nursing the now hibernating Nina in a cardboard box packed with screwed up balls of newspaper.

"We shan't get far at this rate," Nik responded, snow having reduced traffic to a crawl.

"More haste, less speed."

Nik envied his assurance.

"Pity there's no radio-cassette player," Sakhno added. "It'd cheer things up a bit."

"Music? In a hearse?"

"Don't see why not, especially if the corpse was musical. Apart from which, we're not corpses."

As they waited to join the Autobahn, Sakhno conducted a sign-language conversation with Uli, which ended in an exchange of kisses. Nik did his best to be non-existent, immersing himself in the road map, and calculations of time and distance.

After a while Uli took over the driving, and Sakhno lolled yawning beside him, Nina in her box on his knees.

In Liège they bought warm clothing and ate in a Vietnamese restaurant. Nik was surprised at Sakhno's ordering no vodka, but made no comment.

"How far to Luxembourg?" Sakhno asked.

Nik didn't know, but Uli apparently did.

"What does she say?"

"Three hours in this weather, and another hour to Trier. So we can look up Herr Weinberg this evening. And how much shall we touch him for? Two hundred thousand dollars? Half to you, less expenses. And away you go."

"Where will *you* go?"

"We've got a place lined up . . . God, I could do with a drink! But not till we've got ourselves some money."

Coming in sight of the hearse they saw two youths busy doing something at the rear of it. Sakhno darted ahead and knocked one of them senseless. The other fled. The back window was smashed.

After stowing their scattered possessions back in the hearse, Sakhno got Nik to help lift the unconscious youth on board.

"What's the point?"

"He might come in useful."

First a tortoise, now a thief.

66

Sleeping little at night from the discomfort of lying on his back, Viktor spent his days dozing fitfully from exhaustion. Waking from one such doze, he seemed to remember hearing the doorbell and a male voice as well as that of his wife.

"Was that someone at the door?" he asked.

"A man offering to do repairs at a moderate charge. I said we didn't need any repairs. Oh, and he said he could fix an extra aerial for better telly reception."

"And you opened the door to him?"

"You were in the flat, and he'd been everywhere else on the floor."

"What's Yana doing?"

"Playing."

"Don't open to anyone else. I don't think that accident of mine really was an accident."

"An attempt to kill you, do you mean?" she asked in alarm.

"I don't know . . . Just a suspicion. Don't worry. The vital thing is to be more on guard."

Yielding to the temptation of sun and sparkling snow, he went for a hobble round the block, and was encouraged to find his leg no longer hurting, just aching. Sitting on the bench by the entrance and looking round, he spotted a minivan. Miller Ltd Suspended Ceilings. No call for them here in the new blocks. District could do with a few, though. Maybe the driver was local.

At that moment two smartly dressed men emerged from the block, got in and drove away.

That evening Georgiy rang.

"Paris is off, I'm afraid. There's no one to go for, Assistant Military Attaché Kylimnik being no longer with us. Threw himself from an upper window at the Embassy, and to spare embarrassment, into an inner courtyard rather than the street."

"I should have been there, not hanging around Border Troops HQ," Viktor said bitterly.

"In which case there'd have been no defenestration. All things are for the best. Tell you more when we meet."

"When will that be?"

"Plaster comes off tomorrow, right?"

"At three o'clock."

"I'll ring soon after."

"Don't move, lie still for ten minutes. I'll be back," said the doctor, leaving Viktor in screened-off solitude after removing his plaster.

"Glad you're on the mend!" came Georgiy's voice. "Leg OK?"

"Just about."

"Well done! Welcome back to our invisible ranks! Now here's something for you. While you were on watch, we slipped those fine photos of yours to a certain general – the one with a window above the entrance – so that he could study them as well as you. And it worked! He lost his nerve! He had you smashed up, Kylimnik eliminated, then, like a fool, ran straight to those he's in league with. And if they're a bit brighter than him, he'll be the next to fall from a window. They've just the one trump card for all situations, these military types. No finesse. None of the softly-softly approach. Nothing of the chess player about them."

"So do we know who he's in league with?"

"We do, and they're not easily got at – at least not immediately. They're too high up. Our General would seem to be more the trusted executant than one of the strategists. Increasingly, there's a dimension of State Interest. It could be our President who's after the cash. Now, to come back to you and your future. A spell of detached service, I think. First to Saratov. Then further afield."

"Why Saratov?"

"To see Mrs Fourth Man. Her good husband keeps in touch, even when 'on a mission'. You might learn something."

A journey for nothing, Viktor thought, rather wishing he could tell Georgiy what he had already learnt from Refat. Nor did he relish the thought of leaving Ira and Yana alone at this time.

"Where after Saratov?"

"Depends what you come back with. Your London trip set things moving. You must travel more."

"But not to Paris?"

"Paris could yet be on. There are still people of possible future interest there. We'll see. But I'm off. Here's your nice lady doctor coming back. Do what she tells you. Ring you tomorrow."

Viktor sat at the kitchen table, oppressed by the pointlessness of travelling to Saratov and unable to seek advice, except at the unwelcome cost of betraying to Refat the subordinate nature of his own role. It couldn't be worse.

The Miller Ltd minivan parked below prompted thoughts of cracked and flaking ceilings, and reaching for his mobile, he dialled District.

"Duty Officer."

"How's Zanozin?"

"He's better, Comrade Lieutenant. Telling the Major to bring beer. A good sign."

67

With Uli driving, they negotiated the narrow streets of the Old Town of Luxembourg, crossed a deep river gorge by way of a long, red-painted bridge, and at the end of an unlit cul-de-sac, stopped.

"Uli's got a point," said Sakhno, following a sign-language exchange. "We've got to ditch this hearse. So you and Uli wait here. If our Belgian youth surfaces, thump him."

In less than an hour he returned, driving a Volkswagen Passat.

"We'll truss this lad up, stick him in the boot, and off we go. You with Uli in the VW, me following."

Uli drove, clearly familiar with the area and its byways. After a while, she slowed, turned down a narrow farm track, and pulled up at wooden gates bearing a FOR SALE notice. Helped by Uli, Nik lifted the gates off their hinges, opening the way to a yard. Sakhno shut the hearse away in an empty barn, then got behind the wheel of the Passat. Uli sat in the back, nursing Nina in her box.

Twenty minutes later they were back in Germany. This time they drove up to the gates of Weinberg's villa, and then two hundred metres or so along the wall to the right of them, where Sakhno climbed into the now familiar oak.

"No targets. Three windows lighted," he reported returning to earth. "Could be Weinberg's hopped it. We must go and see."

"We've work for you, my beauty," Sakhno said, hauling the unfortunate Belgian out of the boot, freeing his feet but leaving his hands tied. He prodded the youth towards the villa gates, and when they got there, lifted and dropped him over like a roll of carpet. He waited, and when neither dog nor man responded, helped Nik over and nimbly followed.

Crouching, they made towards the house, pushing their prisoner ahead of them. Parked beside the house was the crimson Jaguar, and beside the Jaguar lay the body of a nattily dressed young man, which Sakhno relieved of a still holstered automatic. They then came upon two further corpses with weapons undrawn. Sakhno gave Nik one of the automatics, and pocketed the other.

"Someone's done a good job. Didn't know what hit them."

"Saving us a job."

"We're none of us indispensable!"

Pushing the Belgian through the unlocked door into an unlit

hall, they went up carpeted stairs to a passage, lit by light from a frosted glass door, beyond which a phone rang. Stopping, they listened.

Answerphone sounds followed, then, in good clear Russian, "Ring you in an hour. If no answer, that's it!"

"That was Überkraft," Nik whispered.

Sakhno nodded.

Bursting through the frosted glass door on the heels of the Belgian, automatics at the ready, they found Weinberg slumped in a chair, face as grey as his track suit, a bottle of Johnny Walker spilt on the carpet, where his dropped cigarette was burning a hole.

Stamping out the burn, Sakhno slapped Weinberg in the face.

"You alone?"

Weinberg nodded

"Find the bath, Nik. Fill it with cold water. We must sober him up."

Icy immersion and rough handling by Sakhno helped to loosen Weinberg's tongue.

"What's the money to you, you can't get at it," he said, dabbing his bleeding mouth. "Only the account holders, all three acting together, can do that. If Pierre supplies the password. As Pogodinsky wouldn't. The maximum drawable by any one account holder acting alone is ten per cent."

"Of what?"

"Four billion."

"Bloody hell! A damned sight more than I need! And your pile, where do you keep that?"

"In the bank."

"Where's your cheque book?"

"Desk drawer upstairs."

While Sakhno went to fetch it, Nik raised the unfortunate Belgian to a sitting position from face down on the carpet, where he'd lain since being thrust through the door, and gave him a drink.

Sakhno's apparent lack of interest in the billions came as a surprise. These, surely, were the very funds Ivan Lvovich had sent him, Nik, in search of. Him! It seemed idiotic, ridiculous. But they existed, those funds. And some Pierre had the password for the three – whoever they were – to access them, presumably at a bank. Though how would one draw, how carry away such a sum?

"This four billion, where is it?" he asked Weinberg.

"Cyprus. But it can't be got at."

"Which bank?"

"North Mediterranean."

"Where do I find this Pierre?"

"Aeroflot office, Paris."

As Sakhno came in with the chequebook, Weinberg got to his feet and dragged himself painfully to the table.

"Three hundred thousand DM will do. Endorse it 'Pay cash'."

"Who to?"

"Niklas Zenn."

Sakhno prepared a meal of *tagliatelle*, which Weinberg ate with difficulty, and Nik fed to the Belgian by spoon, Sakhno being unwilling to free his hands.

"What a picture we make!" observed Sakhno. "All we need is an artist!"

A piercing shriek from somewhere overhead intruded on the idyll, prompting Sakhno to reach for the automatic beside his plate.

"Who's that?"

"Nobody. It's my parrot."

"What sort?"

"Collared."

"Does he talk?"

"No."

"Good for him! Why should he talk! He's not a Chinese toy. What's his name?"

"Boris."

"I've got a tortoise called Nina," Sakhno said, as one child might to another.

Again a shriek.

"Go and fetch him, Nik."

Boris was a handsome bird, even the wretched Belgian, who understood not a word, gazed in awe.

"Maybe he's hungry," suggested Sakhno.

Weinberg heaved himself to his feet, crossed to a cupboard, and came back with a tin. The lid had a picture of a white cockatoo.

"You're a better man than I took you for," Sakhno said. "I'm sorry I hurt you. Why not come with us? We could drop you off in Luxembourg."

Weinberg shook his head.

"They'd still hunt me down. They're coming, and I'm not afraid of death. Too damned weary. We're all just pawns."

"You and Nik here, perhaps. Not me. You can stuff your billions. I play a different game," said Sakhno.

Leaving Weinberg and the Belgian to their fate, Sakhno and Nik made their way back to the VW.

Uli was asleep, curled up on the back seat, and as the car moved off, she slept on.

Presenting Weinberg's cheque at the Trier branch of the Deutsche Bank, Nik was surprised and not a little relieved at being paid the sum in notes and finding his pockets able to receive them.

68

SORRY FRIEND'S WIFE TANYA ARRIVING KIEV TODAY 29TH TRAIN 54 MEET ASSIST RE KONCHA = REFAT, said a telegram from Moscow, saving Viktor a fruitless journey to Saratov.

He breakfasted, did his leg exercises, then passed the news of

Tanya's imminent arrival to Georgiy.

"Where've you got this from?"

"We have our sources."

"Wonders never cease! You'd better go and meet her."

Half an hour later Georgiy rang with an address on Khreshchatik Street, where Tanya could stay, and instructions to keep constantly in touch.

In felt tip on the lid of an old shoe-box Viktor wrote TANYA TSENSKY in large capitals.

"Meeting her at the station," he explained to a puzzled Ira.

The duty Zhiguli was waiting in the snow. So, too, the Miller Ltd minivan.

As Viktor stood holding his card up for the stream of passengers to see, a voice at his elbow said, "Kravchenko, not Tsensky, I kept my maiden name," and there she was, petite, in trenchcoat and downy headscarf, pulling a shopping bag strapped to a trolley.

"I've got a car waiting," said Viktor, taking the handle of the trolley.

"They said I'd be met, but I never thought I would be. All I've got is an address, somewhere outside Kiev. I didn't want to come, and they said I shouldn't. But I must find him. We've nowhere to live. It's time our son went to university."

"Who was it told you not to come?" Viktor asked, as they made their way down into the underpass.

"Vasily Gavrilovich and the man with him. Very polite. They helped with money."

Good for Refat, thought Viktor.

"Though whether it will run to a hotel – "

"Don't worry, we've found you a flat. There'll be no charge."

"Thank you! Such kindness!"

Viktor dismissed the driver and himself drove to the address Georgiy had given: Bessarabian Square, Orbit cinema block, second floor. The door was opened by an old lady.

"In you come, tea's ready," she said. "You must be exhausted after two days' travelling."

Parking the trolley in the corridor, Viktor told a now happier Tanya that he would be back in two hours, and that she mustn't leave the flat.

He phoned Georgiy from the car.

"Give her a meal somewhere, then go on to Koncha-on-the-Lakes," instructed Georgiy. "Be there when she talks to the author – maybe he'll remember more than he's said. Make clear, when you bring her back, that she's not to leave the flat."

"I have already."

After a quick snack at McDonald's, Viktor visited Zanozin in hospital.

"What's it like out there?" Zanozin asked.

"Snowy."

"And how's it going?"

"Fast. You could miss the showdown."

"It's two more weeks here, then off to a military sanatorium in Odessa."

"And a high old time with the pensioners!"

"Some hopes! The Major's actually promised me a flat."

"Only to cheer you up, or thinking you unconscious."

"Like an orange?"

"No thanks."

Viktor squeezed Zanozin's hand which was still too weak to be shaken.

"Got the apples, did you?" Valentin asked Viktor, as they sat with Tanya and Svetlana over coffee at the long kitchen table.

"What apples?"

"The ones I gave the fellow you sent with another photo of Nik. Nice chap. Little gold star earring. Strange what you can get away with, now we're a democracy."

"I'll check. But for the benefit of his wife here, could you kindly repeat what you remember about Nik."

"Nothing about the container, then?" she asked at the end of a brief but crystal clear account.

"What container?" Viktor asked in surprise.

"With our furniture and stuff. Left Dushanbe the day before we did."

"No, nothing," said Valentin.

"What size container?" Viktor asked.

"A half, with our piano, sofa, sideboard, ten boxes of books . . ."

"You've got the documentation?"

"In the flat in Kiev."

"We'll check," said Viktor.

"And will you know, by the day after tomorrow, will you know anything by then?"

"I'll see what I can do."

After another round of coffee, Valentin brought up Nik's dollars from their hiding place in the cellar, and with the look of a man glad to shed the responsibility, handed them to Tanya.

69

In Trier they checked in at the Hotel Sheraton, Sakhno announcing it grandly as "his treat".

One uniformed bellboy requested the key to garage the car, another, by gracious sanction of the management, bore Nina up to Sakhno and Uli's bedroom in her cardboard box.

The excellence and luxury of their new surroundings moved Uli to make better provision for Nina. Obtaining a fine wooden box that had contained a dozen of choice French wine, she replaced the rolled-up balls of newspapers, designed to insulate against warmth or excessive cold, with screwed-up tissue paper. It was not until she lifted Nina from her old box to settle her in her new one, that she noticed, lightly scratched into the underside of her shell, V32453H75G.

"Could be the password Pogodinsky was murdered for!" Nik exclaimed. "We're in with a chance! How about giving it a try?"

"And die young? It's an illusion, that sort of money. Think of the effort it cost to get three hundred thousand!"

Sakhno poured vodka. They clinked glasses.

"We're off tomorrow, Uli and I."

"Where to?"

"Where we're not known and shan't be found. Peace and quiet's what's needed for happiness. I'll make a living plying my trade."

"And what's that?" Nik asked, aghast.

But Sakhno, looking singularly acute and sober, empty vodka bottle notwithstanding, ignored the question.

Next morning Sakhno handed Nik seventy-five thousand DM, together with another of the automatics picked up at Weinberg's. The two of them embraced.

"Best of luck, Nik!" Sakhno clapped him on the shoulder. "I expect we'll meet again."

Bag on shoulder, in brilliant sun and cheek-nipping frost, Nik went from the Sheraton to a café for coffee and pastry.

He had nowhere to go, except on in quest of Pierre, and the billions. He smiled at the madness of it. But it was there, somewhere, that money. He knew at least one who was after it, and why – or rather, what it was needed for in Ukraine. Madness, yes, but he was well on the way along a road that had cost Pogodinsky his life, and by now, Weinberg his.

Ordering another coffee, he asked the way to the station.

70

Tanya left on the 08.50 for Saratov, disappointed and depressed at having achieved so little.

Georgiy, rung by Viktor, said that Kiev seemed to have more container depots than chemists, but that he was working on it. And Viktor, hitherto indifferent to how many chemists there were, counted five, driving back to District from the station.

Heavy snow-charged clouds brought darkness earlier than usual. The warm glow of the solitary street lamp below his window, and an unearthly silence broken only occasionally by a car, made New Year, just three weeks off, seem here already.

He thought of Tanya, provincial and mildly foreign in her fluffy head scarf. Odd how concerned she had been about the container, and how little about her husband.

Getting out the Bronitsky file, he looked again at Wojclech's photos. Tsensky's gentle intelligence was in marked contrast to the sharp intensity of Sakhno's. They were like extremes, juxtaposed for contrast: Tsensky involved out of desperation, Sakhno for the sake of money. And where was he, this Tsensky? Still in Germany?

71

The Paris to which Nik came by train was awakening to grey morning: newspaper sellers setting up kiosks, joggers jogging, water carts spraying, shop shutters opening with the swish of katyusha rockets. But there was a café, and amazingly at such an hour, someone sitting reading a paper.

Nik ordered coffee.

"Counter or table?"

"Meaning?"

The *patron* pointed to a slate inscribed "4 francs counter, 8 francs table, 10 francs terrace".

Nik opted for a table.

Lowering his paper, his fellow customer wished him *bonjour*, before raising it to reveal the headline FRENCH BANKER MURDERED IN MOSCOW.

Old habits died hard.

By 10.00 he'd found a cupboard-sized room-with-breakfast in a cheap hotel in the rue de Cléry, and taking one of the street maps provided free, walked, stopping off at two cafés en route, via the boulevards St Denis and de Magenta to the Gare de l'Est, where Tourist Information gave him the address and telephone number of Aeroflot.

Seeing *Izvestiya* and *Kiev Gazette* on sale at a kiosk, he bought a copy of the latter.

The news from Ukraine was not encouraging: miners demanding their last year's wages and picketing Parliament; one corrupt set of government ministers replaced by another; mafia street warfare resulting in dead and wounded; Ukrainian "godfathers" at murdered State Deputy's funeral. On the credit side, Parliament was discussing the financing of General Goloborodko's Ukrainian Federal Bureau.

Life, like his lone, probably vain quest for billions, went on.

Later he took the métro to the Champs Elysées and the Aeroflot office, where, pretending to study the flights on offer, he established that of the five name-tag-sporting males, none was Pierre.

Next day he assessed the female counter assistants at Aeroflot, liked the look of petite, auburn Tatiana, and when she left the office at five that evening, now in a short fox-fur jacket, he was waiting and followed her.

She window-shopped, seeming in no hurry, visited a *parfumerie*, examined lingerie in a boutique, but bought nothing at either. At one of the brightly lit newspaper kiosks she looked at the papers on display, and took a copy of *Moskovskiye novosti*.

"Excuse me, do you speak Russian?" Nik asked, seizing the opportunity.

"I do," she said, pleasantly surprised.

"I've got a map, but I'm lost. Rue de Cléry is what I want."

"Let's go over to that jeweller's, where there's more light."

In the light from the jeweller's Nik began unfolding the map but was soon in difficulty.

"It might be easier to pop into that café and open it on the table," he suggested.

"Good idea."

She quickly marked the route in pencil, after which they sat on over coffee and ice cream.

Tatiana was from Belarus. She and her parents had moved to Moscow after the break-up of the Soviet Union. Her father, formerly a Party worker, had obtained a post at the Ministry of Agriculture, and he had managed to get her a job abroad. She had been here for five months now, since graduating in Germano-Romance Studies at Moscow University. She earned enough to live on and had a tiny one-room flat in Belleville, the Sino-Arabic quarter near Père Lachaise Cemetery. These and other common-place details poured forth as if for the first time in five months, and were eagerly absorbed by a smiling Nik. At last, her own facts exhausted, she asked if he was married.

Nik told of the accident to his wife and son, and for a while they sat in silence. When they next spoke, it was about Paris and people in general. Nik asked what her colleagues were like, but the hoped-for name did not figure.

"Isn't there a Pierre somebody?"

"Tall, small moustache?"

"That's him."

"Tereshchenko. He's Pyotr really but prefers Pierre."

For the first time in his life Nik found himself seen home by a girl.

The rue de Cléry was deserted, and at admirably regular intervals on the opposite side from his hotel stood rubbish bins stuffed with dressmakers' remnants.

"Look, how lovely!" Tatiana cried, pulling out a scrap of material that sparkled in the lamplight. "Lamé. Height of fashion." Folding and slipping it into her handbag, she raised the collar of her fox-fur jacket against a sudden icy blast. "I must be off," she said.

"Do you know the way?"

"I've explored most parts. If I go straight on I get to the boulevard de Sébastopol. From there it's twenty minutes by métro."

"Are you on the phone?"

With the sweetest of smiles, she handed him a card.

Lying in his box of a room, he wondered what exactly had so happily prompted his choice. Her name? Her kind open face? Her attractively big eyes?

Over the *de rigueur* breakfast of coffee and croissant, Nik's thoughts turned to Pyotr Tereshchenko, and the necessity of discovering whether he was in fact Weinberg's Pierre.

That evening Nik took up position under a plane tree where a Moroccan was selling roast chestnuts, and kept watch on the Aeroflot office.

First to emerge were the counter assistants, among them Tatiana, who went her way alone. Ten minutes later several men came out, none of them recognizably Pierre.

Twenty minutes later, there he was: tall, small moustache, long dark raincoat, dark hat, elegant shoulder-suspended leather brief-case. He locked the massive glass door behind him, checked his watch, then set off at a leisurely pace in the direction of the Arc de Triomphe. Nik followed, keeping well back. At Georges V they boarded the same crowded métro, and travelled to an outlying part of the city, where Pierre disappeared into a Chinese restaurant, leaving Nik out in the cold and hungry.

When at long last Pierre reappeared, he was accompanied by a balding, heavily-built man in a sheepskin coat.

"I'll be in touch the moment there's news," the man said, taking leave in the Russian manner and getting into a large Peugeot. He seemed edgy and displeased.

Pierre walked slowly on, as if lost in thought.

Following at a distance on the other side of the deserted street, Nik saw him enter a two-storey house sandwiched between taller buildings. Lights went on in the three downstairs windows, 134 was the number, all he needed now was the name of the street.

Ravenous, he retraced his steps to the restaurant, where a young Chinese divested him of his jacket. With a sense of mission completed, he ordered *canard à l'orange* and a carafe of red, thinking, as he drank, of Sakhno and his "mines".

72

Driving home in the duty Zhiguli, Viktor took it easy as far as Southern Bridge, and was beginning to accelerate on the better sanded surface beyond when a minivan swung into his lane and made straight for him. Viktor swerved, skidded, and struck the barrier, before regaining control. The minivan was the familiar one often parked outside their block.

He slowed, needing time to recover, then, struck suddenly by an appalling thought, drove like a madman.

"Hell of a racket from your place," drooled the drunken neighbour he encountered as he darted from the lift.

Hurling open the door of his flat, Viktor rushed in.

Sprawled on the living-room floor lay a man in an Adidas track suit and spotless trainers. Beneath his left eye, was a bullet hole, and gripped in his dead hand an automatic. And cowering in a corner, terrified, speechless, Ira.

"Where's Yana?"

Ira gestured towards the corridor.

"Have they taken her?"

Ira shook her head.

He found her safe in her pram.

"All right, all right. Daddy's back . . ." he soothed, taking her in his arms and returning her to Ira.

"What happened?"

"He tried to shoot me."

"How did he get in?"

"He was here when I got back from taking out the rubbish."

The dead man had a receiver attached to one ear, and a microphone at the collar of his track suit. In his shoulder holster he had a mini automatic with silencer, and clutched in his plastic-gloved hand was Refat's curious backfirer taken from on top of the cupboard.

He rang Georgiy.

"Go through his pockets."

Reluctantly Viktor obeyed, but found nothing of interest.

"It's a nasty bunch we're up against," said Georgiy. "What you must do now is to put Ira and Yana into warm coats, and drive towards town. I'll phone as you go. What sort of door lock have you got?"

"The standard sort."

"Right. Lock up normally."

Easing the Refat automatic from the corpse's cold grip, Viktor substituted the dead man's own weapon, before conducting Ira and Yana down to the car.

73

Having learnt from Tatiana that Pierre had left unexpectedly for the Midi for a week on business, Nik found himself at a loose end.

A mild, cheek-reddening breeze with a hint of still distant spring did nothing to vary the rhythm of a Paris whose motor horns woke him each morning at the same hour, and whose breakfasts continued with the *de rigueur* coffee and microwave-warmed croissant.

One evening he took Tatiana to a Greek restaurant he liked the look of, where they ate fried octopus, drank chablis, and talked and laughed. It was as if he had left and shed his whole life up to that moment outside in the street. He was light-hearted, in no mood to come down to earth. He had, he felt, fallen for Tatiana, and even more exciting than that, she had clearly fallen for him.

From the restaurant they decided to walk to Tatiana's flat in Belleville. It took them a good hour and a half, and it was getting on for 11.00 before the narrow street became bright with tiny Arab restaurants and cafés, in one of which they paused for coffee and pastries oozing pistachio-and-honey syrup.

Her one-room flat, though small, had an air of comfort that made it seem larger. There was a small reproduction glass-fronted cupboard, a little table, a large pink fabric-covered lampshade diffusing pale, soft light, a broad couch and two bentwood chairs.

They sat in the kitchen at a small round table, drinking wine and talking about nothing in particular, as if to hear each other's voices was all that mattered. At 2.00 in the morning they set about making a salad, and at 3.00 they ate it.

Next morning, after a quick breakfast of coffee and cheese, they set off together, Tatiana all tenderness, Nik buoyed up by the feeling of being wanted and restored to normality. And when the time came for her to dive into the métro, he walked on to his hotel in a state of joyous, emotional weightlessness. He thought of Sakhno's abandoning everything for his blonde Uli. Just as he, Nik, had now no need of anyone except Tatiana. It was all so strange and at the same time natural. He had found happiness, and a shell in which to conceal himself – a beautiful, invisible shell called Paris.

Coming to the Père Lachaise Cemetery, he went in. It had an air of calm, of peaceful happiness, the stones and inscriptions seeming to breathe kindliness, well-being, blissful serenity.

74

For three days Viktor, Ira and Yana had been holed up in an old brick-built house with a glassed-in verandah, on a one-way street in the sought-after holiday suburb of Pushcha-Voditsa. It looked out across a road not to other houses, but to a wood and a view of the lightly frozen lake through leaf-denuded trees.

Ira, now recovered from her recent shock, spent a couple of hours washing the kitchen equipment, old-fashioned crockery and stainless steel cutlery. Judging from the state of the house, no one had lived there for years, but someone had put the water system in order. There was spotless linen in a period cupboard, and in the sitting room, under an embroidered napkin, a Slavutich TV. The kitchen store cupboard contained a stock of tinned fish and tinned peas.

Phoning Georgiy about Miller Ltd, Viktor asked if he might pick up one or two things from the flat, and was told to hang on for a bit, but with no indication of how long "a bit" might be. As to Miller Ltd Suspended Ceilings, there was no such firm in Kiev.

"Was there no phone number?" Georgiy asked.

"No," said Viktor.

The unaccustomed quiet of Pushcha-Voditsa, broken only by the occasional faint familiar clank of a distant tram, was beginning to play on Viktor's nerves.

Sitting on the bench with wrought iron arms outside their wooden shed, he rang District and told Ratko he wouldn't be in for a bit.

"So I'd gathered," was the reply. "And you, by the way, are being 'sought'."

"Who by?"

"The Ministry, so our duty officer says."

At a loss what else to do, Viktor was standing at the gate contemplating the empty road, when, to his surprise, a motorcycle combination ridden by a man in quilted jacket and knitted hat, drew up.

"Viktor Slutsky?" he inquired. "Your mate's broken down at the turn-off. Tipped me five dollars to bring you this box."

The contents, unpacked on the veranda, proved not unlike the rations occasionally received in District: a length of sausage, a jar of mayonnaise, packets of powdered soup, vermicelli, cornflower margarine, etc. There was also an envelope containing the message: "Potatoes in cellar reached via shed – Georgiy."

"The man in the flat," Ira said suddenly as they drank tea after lunch, "I'm sure I've seen him somewhere before, only I can't remember where."

"Try."

For a while they sat in silence.

"Don't worry. It'll come back," Viktor comforted.

And five minutes later it did.

"He was the one who came about a TV aerial!"

That evening Georgiy rang to say that he'd alerted the SVI concerning the minivan, and would keep Viktor informed.

And later there was a TV news flash to the effect that a minivan, probably a Ford Transit, of Miller Ltd Suspended Ceilings, was being sought in connection with a hit-and-run accident, and that anyone sighting it, or aware of its present whereabouts, should ring the SVI on such-and-such a number.

Just short of midnight Georgiy rang again.

"Not in bed, I trust. We've identified your corpse: former parachute captain turned security consultant. Can't say I'm exactly clear, though, as to what occurred. Has Ira said?"

"She doesn't remember."

"Look, I'm not playing investigating officer – just curious. It was a militia issue automatic – presumably yours – he was shot with. And it was Ira who shot him. How exactly did that come about?"

"I'll take it up with her as soon as she's herself again."

"No need. I only wondered whether some other nifty marksman might not have been there. A friend of yours, say."

"No, she was alone."

"Not to worry. Take it easy."

Filled with unease, Viktor threw on a coat and went out.

Complete silence. Not even the clank of a distant tram. Nothing but black sky and a chilly twinkling of stars.

Thinking of London, and Refat and Wojciech, both knowing more than they told, he wished what they knew could be brought together with what he and Georgiy knew. He dialled Refat's Moscow number on his mobile, only to be told, "The number you have dialled is not available".

Two peaceful days followed, and but for the strain he felt under, he could well have been on leave. At times, however, it occurred to him that for his own peace of mind it might be no bad thing to get away completely from the mystery and menace generated by the case.

The dry, snowless weather invested Pushcha-Voditsa with an almost fairy-tale quality.

He pushed Yana for little walks in the wood that lay between them and the river, crunching sere oak and maple leaves underfoot. The few locals they encountered were beginning to wish them good day, and Viktor was beginning to know their faces.

So integral to the silence was the faint echo of trams, that when some time passed without it, Viktor became uneasy – not on account of the trams, but because any break in the barely perceptible rhythm of the place took his thoughts back to Kiev, Nik Tsensky and the body in their flat.

Ira was serenity itself, having discovered in the sideboard a dog-eared copy of Gorky's *Artamonov Affair*. It was not easy going, but in peaceful moments she engrossed herself in it to the exclusion of all else. Looking to see what else the sideboard might hold, Viktor found *War and Peace, Crime and Punishment*, Chekhov short stories, and Shevchenko's *The Minstrel*, and wondered how long it would take her to get through that lot.

"When will it all be over?" Ira asked one evening, when Yana was in bed and they were drinking tea.

"Soon," he promised, "and when it is, we'll go on holiday."

"Summer's the best time for that."

"We'll be finished by then."

At that moment his mobile rang in the pocket of his jacket hanging in the corridor.

"Found your Miller Ltd – in woods near Irpyen. Stripped of equipment, but plainly it's been used for eavesdropping. I sent a bod to check your flat, and he's just reported: two bugs in your corridor, and outside in the hall, there was a mini security camera trained on your door. So all this time you've been appearing on telly. Oh, and another thing. A highly intriguing piece of info. from a neighbour source regarding our German friend. We must meet."

"When?"

"Not going anywhere, are you?"

"Some hopes!"

"Park yourself where I won't wake the house when I ring."

161

It was nearly 1.00 before he did.

"Come forth, listening all the way."

Viktor crept from the house and out through the gate.

"Cross the road, head straight for the lake . . . See the life-saver hut?"

"I think so."

"There's a seat there. Come and join me."

A seat so sheltered from moonlight as to conceal Georgiy's features, but not the fact that he was a good head taller than Viktor.

They shook hands.

"Switch your mobile off, put it away and listen. Nik Tsensky, it appears, is gunning for 'our man in Paris' and I – I'm given quietly to understand – am to see that we get Tsensky before Tsensky gets 'our man'. A bit of a scream, that, coming from a section supposed to be unaware of our doings and our interest in Tsensky. The practical implication is that we are up against someone on our side of the house. Someone in a hurry to knock off Tsensky, now probably hot on the trail of the hoard. Someone smart enough to count on our having a greater interest in finding a live Tsensky to go shares with."

"So?"

"We've no choice, we go ahead as instructed, but alone and to our own agenda. So you've got your dream. You fly to Paris!"

"But I don't speak French."

"You got by in London without English. There are times when it's a plus not knowing the language. Takes them a day to find an interpreter if they pull you in, ample time to think up some cock-and-bull yarn about 'a militia assignment'."

"Why should they pull me in?"

"You might accidentally kill somebody."

"With no gun?"

"A state our people will remedy. But keep them at arm's length, that Paris lot. You don't fraternize, just accept what they say, and go.

If they follow, lead them a dance, get them worried, then lose them."

"Do Ira and Yana stay on here?"

"I think so. We'll move them, if need be. Warn Ira. Tell her, Georgiy will ring."

"There's no phone."

"Tomorrow morning there'll be a phone. Your plane's tomorrow evening. We'll send our taxi."

75

The week went slowly.

By now Nik had spent three nights in Tatiana's tiny flat. They breakfasted and dined together. Each evening he met her punctually from work, and together they leisurely followed some new side-street route from Aeroflot to Sino-Arab Belleville.

On the Wednesday evening, over Turkish coffee in a Turkish restaurant, he plucked up the courage to ask how she would feel about his giving up his hotel room and moving in.

"Of course, especially as you're not earning," was her answer.

"I've money enough for the moment, and I can look for a job . . . I've a German passport."

"German?" she asked in surprise. "You didn't say."

"Does it matter?"

"Of course not. But jobs are scarce. I'll ask around. You've worked as an interpreter?"

"English, German, French."

For a while they sat thinking, Tatiana about jobs, Nik about the imminent return of Pierre and the need to resolve things one way or another: give Security at the Embassy the low-down on the billions, rehabilitate himself, induce Security to forget his existence.

As to the money of dubious origin secreted in his case at the hotel, the sensible thing would be to open an account and bank it the very next day.

On Thursday evening it was a tired, angry Tatiana who came from Aeroflot with no more than the ghost of a smile for her waiting Nik.

"It's been one hell of a day! Let's go for a coffee."

A whole lot of strange Russians had been phoning and asking for Tereshchenko in connection with some mix-up over a pre-paid joint ticket. Tereshchenko was actually due back tomorrow, Friday, but the story they put out had been "not until Monday" to allow him time to think.

Tereshchenko, like Weinberg, was between a rock and a hard place. Maybe that was the reason for his going to the Midi. It was time they talked.

"How about seeing a film tomorrow?" Tatiana asked, suddenly her old self again.

"Tomorrow I've got to meet someone, I'm afraid."

"The day after, then," she said brightly.

76

At 8.00 a white Volga drew up at the gate.

Looking in on Ira and finding her awake, Viktor kissed her goodbye, and she managed a sleepy smile, her grumpiness about his going forgotten.

"When will you be back?"

"I'll ring."

Checking that the car's registration was as Georgiy had said, he threw his bag in the back and was about to sit in the front, when the driver, a severe but intelligent-looking middle-aged man, motioned him to join his bag.

They eased their way out onto the tram-lined road. It was

snowing lightly, and for a time progress was slow. Beyond Berkhovtsy Cemetery, where the road was sanded, they speeded up a little. Intent on the driving, the driver spoke not at all.

Wintery dawn was breaking as they drove through Kiev. Lights were going on, wan silhouettes stepping out on the pavements.

Glimpsing the block of flats that was home, he felt a pang of nostalgia. From the flower-bed roundabout at the end of Kharkov Highway, they took the Borispol road, and after slackening speed for the SVI check-point, continued at a steady 110 kph.

At the airport, the driver took Viktor's bag.

"It's staff gate for us, so you won't need your passport and there'll be no record of your departure," he said, opening an inconspicuous door.

A guard in camouflage combat gear saluted, and pointed to a corridor which brought them out onto the apron.

Drawing up at a boarding tunnel exit was a long squat bus.

"That one's yours," said his driver, handing him a boarding card.

Viktor's ticket was a single, and only when sitting, bag at his feet, on the plane, looking out of the window, did the implications of that strike him. The Tsensky tip-off, as reported by Georgiy, had the appearance of a specially baited trap, but novice as he was, he'd play it hard, this who-eats-who game.

They taxied to the runway, accelerated, and were airborne.

Breaking with the past and hopeful of a future, he met, looking about him, the stare of a thin-faced man with a birthmark on his right cheek. The man looked away, but Viktor felt unsettled for the rest of the flight.

Having only hand luggage, he went straight through to the arrival hall at Charles de Gaulle airport to a young woman displaying his name, who greeted him in Russian, and whisked him away to the car park and a dark green VW Beetle.

"I'll take you to your hotel," she said briskly. "On the back seat you'll find a briefcase with money, and all you need to tide you over."

A silence reminiscent of the dawn drive through Kiev followed.

Dropped at the Etoile de Gallieni, he found his single room modest but comfortable. Sitting on his bed, he examined the contents of the briefcase: a velour-wrapped Beretta, spare magazine, a wad of francs, a street map of Paris, a Russian-language guide, a photograph of Tsensky outside Aeroflot, and another with a cross in biro by the first-floor window of a clearly numbered house in a clearly named street. There was also a visiting card inscribed "Mikhail Zhevelov, Real Estate Consultant", with a mobile number.

As Viktor stared at his own mobile as if in hope of answers, the old-fashioned room phone rang.

"Got everything?" inquired a crystal-clear male Russian voice.

"The briefcase, yes."

"Two hours from now, Subject will be at Aeroflot, Champs Elysées – it's marked on your map – watching the door. See you do a good job."

77

Tsensky was instantly recognizable, standing behind an Arab chestnut seller.

It was nearly 6.00. Aeroflot was shut, most of the staff had left, but lights were still burning.

Viktor positioned himself at a newspaper kiosk some twenty metres off, from which there was a clear view of both Tsensky and Aeroflot.

Animated voices speaking their beautiful but incomprehensible language were filling the broad boulevard. It was Friday evening, and Paris, shop windows aglow, was in weekend mood.

At Aeroflot the display windows dimmed. A tall man in hat and long overcoat came out, locked the door, and headed off in the direction of the Arc de Triomphe.

Tsensky set off after him. Viktor followed.

The street into which they emerged from the métro station was near deserted.

Once the tall man glanced over his shoulder as he walked, almost as if to make sure he was being followed. Finally he stopped to open his gate.

Tsensky darted into the nearest doorway.

Viktor walked boldly on past both Tsensky and the gate.

When Viktor looked back, Tsensky had disappeared.

A man in biker leathers appeared from behind a tree and the glint of his machine, and crossed the road to the gate.

Viktor followed.

The tall man had left the front door slightly ajar, and the biker was now standing with his back to it, listening, until a sudden thud prompted him to investigate, automatic in hand.

A door banged.

Seeing the corridor empty Viktor went in, drawing his Beretta.

"Hands up, Tsensky!" he heard. "Up on your feet, Pierre! You, Tsensky, are dead!"

The moment to intervene had come. Kicking open the door, and seeing Tsensky with his hands raised, Pierre bleeding on the floor, and Biker, swinging to face him, Viktor fired twice.

Biker, dying, tried feebly to turn his weapon on Pierre, but Viktor kicked it away.

Tsensky, having meanwhile retrieved his automatic, now held Victor covered.

"I'm from Kiev," Viktor said uncertainly, by way of explanation.

"To do what?"

"Assist."

"Drop the gun, sit."

Viktor joined Pierre on the floor.

"You were waiting for me, so you know what I want," Tsensky said, addressing Pierre, and receiving no response, struck him in the face with his automatic.

"We'd do better to search," Viktor said quietly.

"Do you know what for?"

"No, but we'll know when we find it."

"Fetch down those books," he ordered Pierre, "and you," he turned to Viktor, "give each one a shake."

"That's not where to look."

"How do you know?"

"Experience."

"As what?"

"CID."

"Which, for God's sake?"

"The Kiev."

"So where would *you* look?"

"Not here."

Motioning them to lead the way, Tsensky followed Viktor and Pierre to the first floor, where there were two bedrooms, a study, a bathroom with jacuzzi, and a storeroom.

"Where shall we start?"

"The study."

Tsensky got Pierre to pull the desk drawers out and pass them to Viktor to examine. Concealed under the last they found an envelope of old Aeroflot cheque stubs for sums ranging from five hundred to a million francs with no indication as to payee.

"Who was this paid to?" Tsensky demanded, and when Pierre gave no answer, struck him again in the face, but to no effect.

"Let me look, Nik, you've had enough," Viktor said gently, and Nik, for whom "enough" did not extend to sustenance, retired with Pierre to the kitchen.

And there, smiling broadly and holding a fat test-tube containing something preserved in liquid, Viktor joined them.

"What is it?"

Viktor laid the corked and sealed test-tube on the table. The waxen, yellow something preserved in liquid was a human thumb.

"Bronitsky's," said Viktor.

"Who's he?" Nik asked Pierre.

Pierre said nothing.

"The man you killed in Kiev," Viktor prompted.

"I killed no one in Kiev," Nik said quietly.

Viktor was inclined to believe him. He didn't look capable of killing anyone.

"Where did this come from?" Viktor asked Pierre.

"It was delivered."

"Where from?"

"Moscow. It should have been collected last week. I thought they'd come while I was away."

"They being?"

Pierre shrugged.

Viktor's mobile rang and he went into the corridor before answering.

"Well?" asked Georgiy.

"We've found Bronitsky's thumb."

"Splendid! Where?"

"At Pierre's, the Aeroflot man. Tsensky's here with me. What now?"

"Still alive, this Pierre? Well, put that to rights, then clear out. Check in somewhere new. With the thumb, of course. Ring you in three hours."

Retrieving his Beretta from beside the dead biker, Viktor returned to the kitchen and shot Pierre dead.

"Now let's get the hell out of here!"

He grabbed the test-tube, and extracting keys from the biker's pocket, ran with Nik from the house.

Physically and emotionally drained, relieved no longer to be taking decisions, Nik climbed pillion behind Viktor.

"Which way's the city?"

"The way we're going."

He had, it occurred to Nik, left his automatic on the kitchen

169

table. No matter, back at the hotel was the one he'd received from Sakhno.

Where he was going, and with whom, he'd no idea.

But there, for a fleeting moment, was the little Chinese restaurant.

78

Abandoning the motorcycle outside a striptease bar on the other side of Paris, they went to a café, where Nik ordered beer.

"After this I'm off," he said.

"Where to?"

"Never you mind."

"I saw your wife," Viktor said. "At Valentin's, when she came to collect the money."

"She's dead. So's my son."

"She wasn't, this time last week."

"Both died in a fire last autumn."

"Who said?"

"Ivan Lvovich."

"She's alive, your Tanya! I met her at the station. I had a card saying 'Tsensky', but she told me she was Kravchenko."

Nik stared incredulously.

Viktor's mobile rang.

"You're where?"

"Some café the other side of Paris."

"With the thumb? Good. Lose that, and your head rolls! Any thoughts re Tsensky? Now he's served his purpose."

"But has he? How about Bronitsky?"

"Bugger Bronitsky! Get rid of Tsensky."

"No!"

"Only joking. He could still have his uses. Find a hotel. Brief you in an hour."

For half Georgiy's hour they sat on over their beer, Nik asking about his wife and her visit to Kiev, as if still unconvinced.

"Here for the night?" asked one of two scantily-dressed girls standing by the hotel reception desk.

Viktor turned uncomprehendingly to Nik, who nodded.

"Shop!" shouted the girl.

A fat man appeared, entered their names in the register, and demanded payment in advance.

No sooner had they shut the door of their double room behind them, than Georgiy rang.

"Fixed up? Right. Now take a shower, rumple the bed, get yourselves to the Gare de Lyon, and catch the express to Lyon. At Lyons airport, collect tickets ready in your names for the 0700 hours flight to Northern Cyprus via Istanbul. Don't, on arrival, have your passports stamped, go for the option of stamp on a separate sheet."

"Then what?"

"You'll be met. Spell of relaxation near Kyrenia. Further details when you're there. Keep close to that thumb!"

"Off we go again," said Viktor, pocketing his mobile.

"Off where?"

"Lyon. Then Cyprus."

"To collect?"

The question came as a surprise. Nik was more in the picture than he thought.

"To relax."

Nik nodded. Not a word so far on the score of Nina's pass number or Weinberg. So the odds were that they, whoever they were, knew nothing about either. Whereas he, having the pass number and knowing which bank, was in the running for ten per cent of four billion!

"I need to phone."

"Do, but don't say where we are or where we're going."

Nik was beginning to warm towards Viktor. He liked his down-to-earthness.

He had to leave Paris for a day or two, he told Tatiana, and would phone the moment he got back. He was minded to mention the cheque book and credit card in the post from the bank, but decided not to in Viktor's hearing.

"My wife, how tall was she?" he asked suddenly.

"Half a head shorter than me – though she may have had high heels."

"Doesn't wear them," said Nik thoughtfully.

79

On the flight from Istanbul, Viktor looked out at distant snow-capped mountains, feeling sadly in need of instructions from Georgiy.

Nik, convinced at last that Tanya and Volodya were alive, struggled to fathom the illogicality of Ivan Lvovich's reporting them dead. In their work, as in the army, illogicality served to camouflage either idiocy or cool calculation, and of the two, the latter seemed the more likely.

As the plane came in over azure, boat-dotted sea to land, Viktor was wondering how to account for the test-tube and contents to customs.

But apart from "Stamp in passport, or separate?" they went through unquestioned.

A young Turk ushered them out to a waiting limousine.

They drove by way of a pleasant mountain road affording glimpses of sparkling sea to the Altinaya Holiday Village. Here they were shown to a chalet.

Viktor went straight upstairs and flopped down on a bed.

Nik investigated the fridge, and was disappointed to find it empty, as would be his future when this affair was over, as it soon would be. Then what? Back to where? Saratov? Kiev? Paris, and naive, wide-eyed Tatiana, to whom he'd grown attached and was missing? A normal life was what he craved, such as, at the moment, was beyond imagining.

A creak from the wooden floor overhead brought his thoughts back to Viktor, whose timely intervention at Pierre's had been not unlike his own "contrived deliverance" of Sakhno. In both cases it had been the result that mattered.

Feeling a sudden urge to talk, he made his way slowly upstairs.

"I'd just like to thank you, Viktor," he said simply.

"Whatever for?"

"Turning up when needed."

"Pure luck. Officially, I was there to protect Pierre from you, but unofficially, to do what I did."

Nik looked uneasy.

"How's dear Ivan Lvovich?" he asked.

"Who?"

"Wasn't it him who sent you?"

"No, someone I only know as Georgiy."

"What happens to me when you've collected the cash?"

"No idea. But something I'd like to ask you is, who was behind the death of Bronitsky?"

"Behind whose death?"

"General Bronitsky, Adviser on Defence to the President. The one whose dead body got sent up on a Coca-Cola balloon."

"And landed on the roof of Security HQ? I heard about that from Ivan Lvovich the day I arrived in Kiev."

"So you were still on the train when Bronitsky died."

"I've still got the ticket somewhere. No, I certainly didn't kill him."

"So you're free to go back to Ukraine or Russia," Viktor said, feeling he was the last person to offer such an assurance.

"Shall we take a walk?"

Half an hour later they came to Kyrenia, a compact little town of pastel-coloured buildings, with few people or cars, and a castle extending into the sea.

"Got a wife?" Nik asked.

"And a daughter. Both at a safe house. There've been attempts to kill us."

"Some would kill a whole city for the sake of four billion."

Viktor looked at him in astonishment.

"Where did you get that figure from?"

"A chap called Weinberg."

They walked on in silence, Viktor grappling with the thought that Nik, like Georgiy, knew more than he, and that Georgiy, in describing Nik's part as played, must know more than Nik.

80

That evening Georgiy rang.

"Thumb in fridge, I take it."

"Actually, no."

"Put it there. It'll keep better. Enjoying your relaxation? You've a first-class sea-food restaurant on the doorstep, how about a slap-up supper? You both deserve one."

In the pleasant, candlelit restaurant, they were shown to a table by the Village Manager himself.

Prawn soufflé, squid in batter, and a medium-dry pleasantly tangy wine, rounded off with Turkish coffee and honey-nut-balls, made an enjoyable and satisfying meal. Once, as they ate, Viktor had the impression that they were being watched by a man sitting alone at a distant table, but put it down to overwrought nerves. The bill, when Nik called for it, was not forthcoming. It had been attended to, the manager informed them, glancing in the direction of the now vacated distant table.

The sky was studded with stars. A warm, gentle breeze rustled the leaves.

"God, what a lovely place!" exclaimed Viktor, but with a note of sadness.

"Why so mournful?" asked a familiar voice, and a grey-suited figure stepped from the shadow of some trees. "Life, for all its difficulties, is good."

"Georgiy!" exclaimed Viktor.

Having shaken hands with Nik, Georgiy suggested that they walk down to the sea.

They made their way in silence, and reaching the beach, sat on a fallen tree. The moon formed a ripply path on the water. Tiny waves lapped the shingle.

"This is where Bronitsky was this time last year," said Georgiy. "Holidaying with some newly made friends."

He paused dramatically.

"The sum withdrawable by Bronitsky alone, as opposed to in concert with two old friends of his, blissfully unaware what he was up to, struck these new friends as inadequate. So back he goes to Kiev to persuade the other two to join in the withdrawal, the intention being then to disembarrass himself of them. All, perhaps, against the promise of the premiership, though not much of a return against the billions involved. Bronitsky bit off more than he could chew."

"And so you killed him?" Viktor challenged.

Staring impassively out to sea, Georgiy hurled a pebble.

"Bronitsky died of cognac and tablets he ought not to have taken with alcohol, thereby leading us a dance. What happened between his leaving the restaurant and becoming airborne, I don't know, nor does it matter. For a day or so, while we complete his business for him, he'll still be with us in a sense."

Nik's thoughts were elsewhere. He was trying to imagine becoming reunited with Tanya, and finding it impossible. It was as if the very possibility had been blocked by his acceptance of her death.

"Thinking of her, Nik?" Georgiy inquired out of the blue, passing him a snapshot. It showed Tanya about to board a train, and as could be seen even by moonlight, plainly unhappy.

"Taken at Kiev."

"Who by?" asked Viktor.

"Those charged with your safety."

He heaved himself to his feet.

"Come, let's hit the road for Altinaya. I'll relieve you of the thumb, you can relax, and the day after tomorrow it's back to work."

Nik showed surprise. Viktor concealed his.

High over the mountains a meteorite shot into nothingness.

81

"That thumb," said Viktor, as the three of them sat next morning in Kyrenia over a glass of beer on the sea promenade, "what are you going to do with it?"

"Tomorrow you'll see," said Georgiy.

Disinclined to think that far ahead, Nik found himself envying Sakhno in hiding with Uli, but almost certainly enjoying life.

They lunched at Georgiy's expense and largely in silence, in a little fish restaurant, and by 5.00 were back in Altinaya sitting over wine and coffee.

"Take it easy for the rest of today," was Georgiy's fatherly parting advice. "Have an early night. Big day tomorrow. I'll call for you at 8.00."

Nik lay on his back contemplating a ceiling dappled with light from the narrow window. This abrupt removal to Cyprus left him unmoved. After Tanya and Volodya's return from the dead nothing could surprise him. But having lived their deaths, it was not easy to rejoin their lives. Having been buried with them, it was as if he had ceased to exist for them.

"You asleep?" he asked turning to Viktor.

"No."

"Ever go camping with the Pioneers when you were a kid?"

"No."

"I did. Three times. This is like a fourth."

"How so?"

"There was a game we had. Summer Lightning. Sort of treasure hunt. I don't remember exactly. What I do remember is how one evening we'd be told, Summer Lightning tomorrow! And how excited we'd be, not knowing what to expect, but expecting it to be fun. You're like that as a kid."

"And now it's the same?"

"Expecting it to be fun, yes," Nik said, but with a note of uncertainty that implied the opposite.

Viktor made no response. He, too, was staring at the ceiling.

A motorcycle roared past outside.

"So tomorrow it's the big one," Nik said calmly. "After which we're disposable. Not that I feel of any bloody use to anyone any more."

Again no response from Viktor.

Georgiy arrived at 8.00 in summery flannels, dark blue shirt and grey jacket, and carrying a briefcase.

"All fit?" he inquired, leading them out to a Suzuki mini-jeep.

"Fifteen dollars a day, petrol extra. It's peanuts what they charge for these things here."

Viktor sat beside Georgiy, Nik in the back.

"This is where we collect, is it?" Nik asked abruptly.

Georgiy smiled into the mirror.

"Yes. The big money."

Seeing how tiny the mini-jeep's boot was, Nik wondered where they would put it.

A mobile rang. Viktor reached for his, but Georgiy forestalled him.

"Be there in an hour . . . All set this end . . . Suzuki jeep, brownish yellow. OK. At the Karpas Peninsula–Famagusta fork we slow."

Pocketing his mobile, Georgiy produced automatics.

"You're my bodyguards . . ."

At the fork, where Georgiy slowed, a chocolate-coloured Mercedes eased out behind, and as they accelerated, fell back.

Famagusta seemed larger, livelier, busier than sleepy Kyrenia, and Georgiy appeared to know the place. At the flower-bedded, Atatürk statue roundabout, he swung right and brought them to a hotel overlooking the lifeless, war-scarred buffer zone between the Turkish sector and the Greek.

They made their way out onto a terrace facing the sea, and Georgiy ordered coffee.

"From this point on, questions are out," he said. "Understood?"

They nodded.

Georgiy consulted his watch.

"We'll be joined shortly by someone else for you to protect."

"Is danger anticipated?" Viktor asked.

"Not at the moment, though anything's possible. After which, no more questions!"

They drank their coffee in silence, Georgiy looking now at his watch, now around at the other customers, now at a ship on the horizon.

Someone came and sat at the table next to theirs. Georgiy greeted him with a smile. The newcomer, Viktor saw to his astonishment, was Refat.

"Good morning." He looked pleasantly at each in turn, and as a waiter appeared ordered a coffee in English. "We leave in twenty minutes," he said. "It's fifteen minutes from here to the bank. We're expected."

"And you two keep close behind, eyes peeled," Georgiy threw in.

At the bank, an Arab official took five copies of a document from a leather folder and laid them out on his desk, open at the last page.

Georgiy made an ink impression of his right thumb on each document in the appropriate place, and Refat did the same. The Arab, who had shown him the greater deference throughout, wiped Refat's thumb clean with ink solvent before turning to Viktor and Nik, assuming one of them to be next. At which point Georgiy, having pulled on surgical gloves, produced the thumb, and the Arab supervised the imprinting as unconcernedly as if it were still part of a person.

When the three thumb-signatures had been computer-scanned and checked, prints were taken of Viktor's right-hand index finger and Nik's right-hand thumb. These were then scanned into the computer together with each of their passport photographs.

Outside in the brilliant sunlight, Georgiy tossed Viktor the keys of the jeep, and travelled with Refat in the Mercedes.

"You all right?" Viktor inquired after they had driven for ten minutes in silence.

"Bit tired," Nik confessed, then added, "You know this Refat chap, do you?"

"Yes, why?"

"I was thinking of a pal of mine in Africa, who drove over a mine."

"No chance of that here."

"How about an in-car bomb? Stop and have a look?"

"Georgiy said keep close behind."

"So we wouldn't stop and look."

"Then why all that stuff with our fingerprints and photos?"

"Means nothing. Things can be kept in test tubes."

Viktor found Nik's unease infectious, and the more so since the

179

out of the blue arrival of Refat. If Georgiy had all along been hand in glove with Refat, why all the nonsense of his having to conceal from Georgiy his own connection with Refat?

"And where the hell is this cash they've just signed for?" Nik persisted.

"No idea."

They had now left the town behind. On one side, meadows; on the other, barbed wire of some military installation.

"Does your wife know where you are?" Nik asked suddenly.

"Look, Nik, if you were expendable, you'd have been expended in Paris."

"Seems we're heading for the airport," Nik said, as a plane flew over very low – dark thoughts apparently allayed.

The Mercedes pulled into the side, Viktor drew in behind. Georgiy came round to Viktor's window.

"Let's have the guns."

Meekly they handed them over.

Producing a duster, Georgiy wiped both weapons free of prints, and tossed them into the roadside grass.

"That's it," he said, smiling broadly. "So on and up we go!"

82

From Ercan they flew to Istanbul, from Istanbul to Rome, and from Rome to Larnaca in the Greek sector of Cyprus, morale much improved by the excellence of the in-flight catering enjoyed on the final leg of their journey.

From Larnaca airport they were driven to Limassol and the offices of Kostakas & Co., where they were received by Zakhariya, clearly an old friend of Georgiy's.

"All set, then, at this end?" Georgiy asked in English.

"Of course! We're the best."

Cinnamon-scented coffee was served by Zakhariya's charming daughter, and for a while they sat in silence.

"Just one small thing, Georgiy," Zakhariya began unctuously, "storage charges have gone up a little."

"And it's payment in advance."

Zakhariya nodded.

"How much?"

"Half a million would cover it."

Georgiy and Refat exchanged glances.

"You really are all set to load?" Refat asked.

"We are," smiled Zakhariya. "Slick as a Swiss bank, that's us."

Refat drew one of Zakhariya's phones towards him.

"Per Western Union," Zakhariya prompted, with a smile which broadened as Refat authorized Moscow to pay.

At the vast dockside container warehouse Zakhariya reached down one of the cartons, with which Refat's container was packed, stripped back the sticky tape, and stepped aside for Georgiy to examine the bundles of hundred-dollar notes it contained. Refat declared himself satisfied, the warehouse manager re-sealed and replaced the carton, then closed and re-sealed the container.

"See it loaded, and accompany it on board," Georgiy ordered Nik and Viktor.

"On board what?" Viktor asked.

"Container Ship *Lisichansk*. Ukrainian flag."

They saw the container loaded, then sat guard on thoughtfully provided plastic chairs. Hot food was delivered to them.

"Do you know," said Nik suddenly, "I was supposed to get a family flat in Kiev on the strength of reclaiming this money. Plus a job in Security."

"Meaning what?"

"A sort of Ukrainian Federal Bureau, a new idea Parliament refused the funds for. So my Ivan Lvovich said."

"There actually is a new National Investigation Bureau."

"Is that what you are?"

"Wish I was. No, I'm just militia."

Refat and Georgiy appeared shortly after dark, accompanied by the ship's captain.

Refat broke the seal and opened the container.

"That's the one," said Georgiy, pointing to the carton opened at Limassol.

Refat lifted it down.

Opening the carton, Georgiy handed Viktor and Nik ten bundles of notes each, then turned to the captain.

"There's eight hundred thousand dollars there for you. And you can come with us if it's a question of dodging Ilichovsk customs, and we'll put you ashore at Istanbul."

"No sweat," said the captain. "We can hide anything up to a tank."

Refat closed the doors.

"Come, you two," said Georgiy. "We're leaving ship."

They followed him to the side. Bobbing below they saw a trim motor yacht.

"You're leaving all that money, just like that?" Viktor asked Refat as they waited for Georgiy to climb down the ladder.

"What we're leaving is a container of contraband cigarettes, shortly to be escorted by our own brave Navy to the Black Sea port of Ilichovsk. Come on, down you go."

Two hours later Dimitris, the swarthy Greek skipper, brought his yacht alongside Grozny, a towering container ship, port of registration Novorossiysk, hove to with engines silent.

"Decision time," Refat announced, joining Viktor and Nik drinking coffee with Dimitris in the cabin. "Georgiy and I are sailing on Grozny to Novorossiysk, and can do without you for the time being. Dimitris will be happy to land you at Piraeus, and from there you can make your own way."

"Why Novorossiysk, when the money's for Ukraine?" Viktor asked in surprise.

"The money's for Russia," said Refat, "to set against the Ukrainian debt for natural gas. All by agreement with the future government. The present Kiev bunch would only blow it on getting re-elected. Better our way, don't you think?"

Viktor ignored the question.

"Kiev for me," he said firmly.

"As I expected," said Refat. "So come with us to Novorossiysk, and travel home from there. How about you, Nik?"

Nik said nothing.

"We'll call further on your services," Refat continued. "And we'll see you safe. After all, we've you and Viktor to thank equally for the recovery of four billion. So where's it to be?"

"Paris," Nik said quietly.

"I've a fax here that could change your mind," Refat said, passing it to him.

Above the letterhead, a tiny picture of Sakhno and Uli seated on the bonnet of the familiar hearse before the premises of Sachs Funerals.

"Hi, Nik!" read the message. "Congrats on striking oil. Into undertaking here, in Prague. No shortage of clients! Could do with an assistant. Care to join me? Go for a drive? I'm at 18, Marcel Popelar Street. Tel. 134-53-64."

Nik stowed the fax away in the breast pocket of his denim suit.

"Well?"

"Piraeus, please."

"Good man!" said Refat. "Regards to Sakhno! You know each other's ways. Build on it."

"Right," he said, turning to Viktor, "you and I had better go on board."

Nik and Viktor embraced.

"Slip Dimitris a couple of thousand when you land," Refat

advised Nik. "And hang on to that American Express card. Could come in useful. Take it as a present from Ivan Lvovich."

"Who's where?"

Refat shrugged.

"Hiding abroad. The National Investigation Bureau got going without him. Anyway, he'd never have made it to the money. It's amazing how you did. *Au revoir!*"

As *Grozny*'s engines throbbed into life, Dimitris' yacht swung sharply away.

Nik sat alone in the cabin lost in thought. One day perhaps, when he was clear where home was, he'd return there. He needed time – a month, a year, maybe, to think.

Meantime he would take that job with Sachs Funerals. From Prague he could visit Paris, write to Saratov, send Tanya and Volodya money to buy a fine flat and be not too angry. Dear to him as they were, *he* was no longer the same man. Time was needed to mend, make good the distortion inflicted by life.

But now for Piraeus.